The Women

Ben Porcelli

DEDICATION

The novel **"The Women"** centers on the intertwined lives of three women from different backgrounds and generations, each facing their unique challenges and triumphs. Set in a picturesque coastal town, the story explores themes of friendship, identity, and resilience..

CONTENTS

CHAPTER 1:

A NEW DAWN

Eleanor stood motionless at the threshold of the kitchen, her gaze fixed on the empty chair at the far end of the table. The morning sun streamed through the bay window, casting a warm glow that used to highlight his silver hair as he sipped his morning coffee. Today, the chair was just a silhouette against the brightening day, a stark reminder of his absence.

It had been three weeks since the funeral. The sympathies had dwindled, the comforting arms had retracted, and the hum of daily life had resumed for everyone but her. In this newfound silence, the house seemed to echo with memories, each room whispering stories of the years they had shared.

Eleanor shuffled to the coffee maker, her slippers scuffing softly against the tile. The routine was deeply ingrained, almost mechanical. One scoop of coffee, two cups of water—habits formed over decades of marriage, now halved by necessity but not by choice. As the coffee brewed, the familiar bitter aroma filled the kitchen, momentarily warming the void in the air.

With her cup in hand, she wandered into the living

room, settling into the plush embrace of her reading chair. The book on the end table lay open, bookmarked and untouched since the day he had gone to the hospital. She stared at it, pondering whether to pick it up or leave it as another relic of the past.

The quiet was suddenly interrupted by a chirp from her phone—an alert for today's date. It was her calendar reminding her of an event she had set months ago: "Visit the Seaside Art Gallery, new exhibition opens." She had forgotten about it amidst the flurry of the last few weeks.

Eleanor contemplated the idea. It had been ages since she'd done something cultural without him, without having to consider if he'd enjoy the outing or if the walking would be too much. A part of her resisted the change, longing for the comfort of familiar routines, while another, more subdued part, urged her to step out, to embrace the parts of herself that had lain dormant.

With a slow, determined breath, she stood up, placing the coffee cup in the sink. Today, she decided, would be different. She went upstairs to dress, choosing a light blue blouse and her favorite pearl earrings—small tokens of normalcy and perhaps, a touch of defiance against the grief that threatened to engulf her mornings.

As Eleanor drove to the gallery, the streets of her

2

coastal town unfolded with the promise of early summer. The air was crisp, laced with the tang of salt and blooming wildflowers. She rolled down the windows, letting the sea breeze sweep through the car, tousling her hair and clearing the cobwebs of isolation.

Arriving at the gallery, Eleanor paused at the entrance, her hand hovering over the door. This act of walking in alone felt monumental. But as she stepped into the cool, quiet space of the gallery, she realized that the weight of solitude was perhaps, just for a moment, a bit lighter. The walls were adorned with vibrant canvases, each piece a burst of color that beckoned for her attention, coaxing her further in.

As she moved from one painting to the next, Eleanor felt a stir within her, a whisper of the woman she used to be before life had asked her to be nothing more than a partner and caregiver. Today, amidst the art and the echo of her own footsteps, she began to remember that woman.

Eleanor's journey of rediscovery had just begun, under the watchful eyes of painted figures and landscapes that seemed to understand the language of loss and hope. Here, in the quiet solitude of the gallery, Eleanor found the first threads of a new beginning, woven subtly into the tapestry of her new life.

CHAPTER 2:

CROSSROADS

Mia sat in the conference room, the glow of her laptop screen illuminating her face with an eerie blue light. Around her, the walls were adorned with the latest digital innovations—a stark contrast to the timeless art Eleanor had surrounded herself with just a few miles away. The room was filled with a palpable tension, as Mia prepared to lead the weekly tech team meeting.

At thirty-four, Mia was a lead product manager at NovaTech, a cutting-edge software company that specialized in AI and machine learning. Her role was crucial, bridging the gap between the developers' technical expertise and the executive team's strategic goals. Today, however, was different. She was to pitch a new project that could revolutionize the company's approach to data privacy—a passion of hers, but a contentious issue within the higher ranks.

As her team members filed in, Mia reviewed her notes one last time. She knew her proposal was a gamble; privacy was often sacrificed for the sake of innovation in the tech industry. But she believed in the potential for a balance, and this project could prove it.

"Good morning, everyone," Mia began, her voice steady despite the flutter of nerves. "Today, I want to discuss something that could change the playing field for us regarding consumer trust and data handling."

She clicked to the first slide, a bold statement emblazoned across the screen: 'Privacy-First: A New Paradigm'. As she delved into the technicalities and potential market impacts, Mia could feel the room's temperature shift—skepticism mixed with intrigue.

Jason, the CTO, raised his hand. "Mia, while I appreciate the innovation here, aren't we risking slowing down our development cycles? Our competitors aren't exactly waiting for us to catch up."

Mia nodded, expecting this. "True, Jason. However, consider the long-term trust we could build with our users. It's not just about speed; it's about sustainability and ethics in tech. We have a chance to lead, not just compete."

The meeting stretched on, with every point Mia made met with a counterpoint. Yet, as the discussion wound down, she felt a cautious optimism. She had planted a seed, and now it needed time to grow.

Exhausted but invigorated, Mia packed up her things as the conference room emptied. She needed a break, a moment to clear her head. On impulse, she decided to visit the Seaside Art Gallery. Art was her refuge, a world away from circuits and code.

As Mia stepped into the gallery, her eyes adjusted to the softer light, and her paced breathing slowed. The vibrant colors and expressive brushstrokes on display contrasted sharply with the sterile precision of her work environment.

Wandering through the gallery, Mia stopped in front of a particularly striking painting. It depicted a turbulent sea under a stormy sky, the waves captured in mid-crash, powerful and unyielding. It resonated with her, reflecting the turmoil she felt in her professional life, caught in the push and pull of innovation and integrity.

Lost in thought, she barely noticed the older woman standing nearby, her eyes also fixed on the painting. It was Eleanor, though the two had yet to meet. Eleanor turned to Mia, sensing her deep contemplation, and smiled.

"It's captivating, isn't it?" Eleanor said softly. "The way the artist has captured the chaos and beauty of the sea—it's like life, always in motion."

Mia turned, surprised by the comment but appreciative. "Yes, exactly. It feels a lot like the decisions we face—never easy, often messy, but beautiful in their potential."

The two women shared a moment of understanding, an unspoken connection forged by their mutual appreciation of the art. Unbeknownst to them, this chance encounter at the gallery would be the first of many, each meeting strengthening the bond between them, as their paths converged at this unexpected crossroads.

CHAPTER 3:

ESCAPE TO SAFETY

S ophie's hands trembled slightly on the steering wheel as she navigated the winding roads that led to the coastal town. The car was packed with everything she could fit into it—clothes, art supplies, a few cherished books, and her old, slightly out-of-tune guitar. Her rearview mirror was intentionally angled away so she couldn't see what she was leaving behind, only what lay ahead.

At twenty-six, Sophie was starting over, running not just toward something, but also away from someone—her ex-boyfriend, whose charm had darkened into control and fear. The decision to leave had come one night after a particularly frightening argument, and now, with every mile she put between herself and her past life, she felt a mix of fear and relief.

The town appeared on the horizon just as the sun began to set, casting a golden glow over the quaint homes and shops that dotted the landscape. Sophie had chosen this place because of its vibrant local art scene and its reputation as a peaceful, welcoming community—a stark contrast to the chaos she had fled.

She pulled up to a small rental cottage she had arranged online, its white picket fence and blooming roses promising a semblance of the tranquility she desperately sought. The cottage was small, just one bedroom, but it was hers, and it was safe.

After unloading her car, Sophie walked down to the beach, feeling the cool sand between her toes. The ocean was vast and soothing, its rhythmic waves a comforting backdrop to her tumultuous thoughts. She let out a long breath, allowing the sea breeze to clear her mind.

That night, as Sophie unpacked her art supplies and set up a makeshift studio in the corner of the living room, she felt a spark of something that had been missing for a long time—hope. Her paintings had always been her refuge, a way to express what words could not. Now, they would be her voice in this new chapter.

In the days that followed, Sophie threw herself into the local art community. She attended gallery openings, participated in art workshops, and gradually began to share her work. It was at one of these events, a community art fair, where she met Eleanor and Mia.

Eleanor was immediately taken with Sophie's vibrant use of colors and the raw emotion in her pieces. She introduced herself and Mia, who was equally impressed. The three women chatted about art, life, and the unexpected journeys that brought them to where they were.

For Sophie, meeting Eleanor and Mia felt like the first real connection she'd made in a long time. They offered no judgment, only understanding and a shared appreciation for the beauty of expression, whether through art or life itself.

As the fair wound down, Eleanor invited Sophie to join them for coffee the next weekend. "There's something special about sharing time with those who appreciate the finer things in life, like good art and even better company," Eleanor had said, her invitation warm and genuine.

Sophie accepted, her heart lighter than it had been in months. That evening, as she walked back to her cottage under a starlit sky, she realized that perhaps this town, and these new friends, could really be her sanctuary, a place where she could heal and grow, surrounded by the sea and souls that understood the art of starting over.

CHAPTER 4:

FIRST ENCOUNTERS

The following Saturday, the quaint café near the Seaside Art Gallery buzzed with the gentle hum of weekend chatter and the clinking of coffee cups. The walls displayed an eclectic mix of local art, providing a backdrop that encouraged conversation and contemplation. It was here, surrounded by the aroma of freshly brewed coffee and pastries, that Eleanor, Mia, and Sophie met for their planned coffee date.

Eleanor arrived first, choosing a table near the window that offered a view of the ocean. Her early arrival was intentional; she wanted a moment to soak in the environment, a middle ground between her past and her potential future. As she sipped her cappuccino, she reflected on the surprising turn her life had taken since visiting the art gallery. Making new friends was not something she had anticipated at her age, yet here she was, eager and a bit nervous.

Mia walked in next, her brisk, purposeful stride slowing as she scanned the café and spotted Eleanor. She greeted her with a warm smile, the kind that reached her eyes and eased the slight apprehension she felt about mingling her personal and professional lives. "Eleanor, it's so good to see you again," Mia said as she sat down, placing her artisanal tea on the table. "This place is charming."

"Not as striking as your tech world, I imagine," Eleanor replied, her tone playful yet genuinely interested.

"You might be surprised," Mia chuckled. "Sometimes, it's good to step away from the screens and see the world in its true colors."

Sophie arrived just moments later, her artistic flair evident in her attire—a vintage floral dress paired with a denim jacket, her hair pulled back in a loose bun. She carried a sketchbook, which she clutched like a lifeline. "Hi, Eleanor, Mia," she greeted, her voice carrying a hint of nervous excitement. "Sorry I'm a bit late. I got caught up finishing a piece."

"No worries at all, Sophie," Eleanor reassured her, gesturing to the seat beside her. "We're just glad you could make it."

As they settled into a comfortable rhythm of conversation, the trio shared stories about their lives. Eleanor talked about her teaching career and the years she spent nurturing young minds. Mia discussed the challenges and triumphs of being a woman in a high-tech environment, her passion for her work evident in every word. Sophie, though more reserved, opened up about her journey as an artist and the therapeutic nature of her work.

The conversation soon turned to deeper, more personal topics. Mia revealed her struggles with balancing her demanding career with her desire for a personal life. "It's like I'm always on a tightrope, trying to not fall into neglecting one for the other," she admitted.

Sophie nodded in understanding, then shared her recent escape from an abusive relationship, a revelation that brought a solemn air to the group. "Art helped me cope. It was my escape, my way to communicate when words failed me," she explained, her eyes not meeting theirs.

Eleanor reached out, covering Sophie's hand with her own. "You're very brave, Sophie. And you're not alone. We all have our battles, hidden behind the facades we present to the world."

The initial awkwardness melted away, leaving a newfound closeness. They talked about everything from favorite books and films to philosophical debates on ethics in technology and the importance of art in society. It was clear to all three women that this meeting was the beginning of something significant—a friendship that would offer each of them the support and understanding they craved.

As they parted ways, they made plans to meet again, each woman feeling a bit more connected, a bit less isolated in their individual struggles. They had stumbled upon a rare kind of friendship, one that promised to deepen with each shared experience and every heartfelt conversation.

CHAPTER 5:

EVENING AT THE BEACH

A s the late afternoon sun dipped toward the horizon, casting a golden glow over the coastal town, the three women met at the local beach, each carrying the unspoken hope that this casual gathering would cement the budding friendships they had started to cherish. The beach, with its rhythmic waves and salty breeze, seemed the perfect setting for a relaxed evening.

Eleanor arrived first, a large beach blanket tucked under her arm and a cooler filled with refreshments trailing behind her. She chose a spot near the water, where the sand was soft and the sound of the waves most soothing. As she spread the blanket and arranged the cooler, her movements were meticulous, reflective of her years of organizing school picnics.

Mia was next, her steps quick and eager. She brought with her a wireless speaker and a playlist she had thoughtfully put together— a mix of jazz, soft rock, and acoustic covers. "I thought some music might complement the sunset," she said, her voice carrying a note of excitement.

Sophie carried her sketchbook and a small box of pastels, her artist's eye already capturing the changing colors of the sky and sea. "I might try to catch some of these colors. They're just too beautiful to ignore," she confessed, a shy smile playing on her lips as she settled down beside Eleanor.

With the scene set, the women lounged on the blanket, their conversation flowing as freely as the wine they sipped. They shared stories of their younger days—Eleanor's mischievous college adventures, Mia's early days navigating the tech world, and Sophie's spontaneous road trips that fueled her art.

As the sun began to set, painting the sky in hues of orange, pink, and purple, Mia turned the music down and suggested, "How about we each share something we haven't told anyone else before? It could be a fear, a dream, something we're proud of—anything really."

Eleanor nodded, the reflective light in her eyes hinting at the depth of her life's experiences. "I'll start," she offered. "When I was young, I dreamt of being a dancer. I was actually quite good, but life... well, it took a different turn. Sometimes, I wonder what would have happened if I'd pursued it."

Mia listened intently, then shared her own confession. "I'm scared of never finding someone who understands the demands of my career. I worry that love might always take a back seat to my ambitions."

Sophie's admission came more hesitantly. "I'm afraid of him finding me. My ex, I mean. Even being here, sometimes I wake up thinking it was a mistake to try and start over. But then, I have days like this, and it feels like maybe, just maybe, I made the right choice."

Their revelations brought them closer, weaving threads of vulnerability and trust into the fabric of their friendship. The air grew cooler as the sun disappeared below the horizon, but the warmth between them remained.

As they packed up to leave, Eleanor paused, looking at Mia and Sophie. "Thank you, both of you. Tonight has been... it's been wonderful."

Mia smiled, her earlier worries momentarily forgotten. "It has, hasn't it? Let's not let this be the last time."

Sophie, feeling more anchored to this new place and these new friends, agreed. "It won't be. We should make this a tradition."

Agreeing to meet again soon, they left the beach under a twilight sky, the stars just beginning to twinkle in the peaceful expanse above. Each woman carried with her a sense of belonging and a faint echo of the ocean's timeless song, a reminder of the evening they shared and the promise of many more.

CHAPTER 6:

HIDDEN DEPTHS

I n the days that followed their evening at the beach, Eleanor found herself revisiting the old dream she had shared—dancing. The thought, once buried under years of other priorities, now stirred within her with a new vigor. Encouraged by her newfound friendship and their shared confessions, she decided to enroll in a beginner's dance class specifically designed for seniors, held at the local community center.

As Eleanor entered the dance studio, a mix of nerves and excitement buzzed through her. The room was filled with people around her age, some more agile, others just as hesitant. The instructor, a lively woman in her fifties named Carol, welcomed her with a warm smile. "We're all here to find our rhythm again," Carol said, a statement that resonated deeply with Eleanor.

Meanwhile, Mia faced depths of a different kind. Inspired by their heartfelt discussion, she began to contemplate how she might bring more personal fulfillment into her life, beyond the confines of her demanding career. She started by revisiting her old blog, which she had set aside due to her hectic schedule. It was a space where she once shared her thoughts on technology, ethics, and female empowerment—a passion project that brought her a sense of purpose.

Deciding to revive the blog, Mia spent her evenings researching and writing her first post in months. It was about the intersection of technology and privacy, inspired by the project she was championing at work. Publishing it felt like a step towards balancing her professional ambitions with her personal voice.

Sophie, motivated by the security she felt with Eleanor and Mia, took a significant step in her artistic journey. She began working on a new series of paintings that explored themes of fear and freedom, a reflection of her recent escape and new beginnings. Each stroke was a testament to her resilience, each color a part of the story she was now ready to tell.

One afternoon, the three women met at Eleanor's house for tea. Eleanor shared her experience at the dance class, her eyes alight with excitement. "It's liberating, dancing again. I had forgotten how much joy it can bring, how it frees something inside you."

Mia, too, shared her latest blog post, passing her tablet around so Eleanor and Sophie could read it. "It's been too long since I wrote something just because I wanted to," she admitted. "It feels good to share my voice again, not just my skills."

Sophie unveiled a canvas she had brought with her, one of her new pieces. It depicted a woman standing on a cliff edge, looking out over a tumultuous sea beneath a breaking storm. "This is how I've felt—on the edge but ready to face the storm," she explained, her voice steady but full of emotion.

Their shared endeavors and vulnerabilities created a deeper bond between them. They recognized parts of themselves in each other's stories, and this recognition fostered a profound sense of solidarity and support.

As the afternoon waned, they agreed to make these gatherings a regular occurrence, each meeting a chance to share parts of their lives they seldom showed the world. For Eleanor, Mia, and Sophie, these get-togethers were not just about friendship; they were a lifeline, a way to navigate the complexities of their lives with the support of those who understood.

CHAPTER 7:

TECH TROUBLES

Mia was sitting in her home office early one morning, her eyes glued to her laptop screen. The soft hum of her high-powered computer was usually a comforting background noise, but today it was punctuated by the incessant pinging of incoming emails and alerts. The digital environment she thrived in was in chaos, a cyberattack having hit NovaTech overnight.

The attack had compromised some of the company's data, and as a lead product manager with a focus on security, Mia was right in the thick of the response. Her home office was littered with coffee cups and notes, evidence of her hours-long effort to coordinate with her team and manage the crisis.

"Mia, we need your guidance on the encryption

vulnerabilities," came a voice from her laptop's speaker, breaking her concentration. It was Derek, one of the senior developers.

"Right, let me pull up the latest reports. We might need to push a patch faster than we thought," Mia responded, her fingers flying over the keyboard, pulling up data and code repositories.

As she worked, her mind was a whirl of strategies and countermeasures, but another part of her was calculating the personal cost of this crisis. She had planned to spend the weekend visiting a local art exhibit with Eleanor and Sophie, a welcome break that now seemed unlikely.

Hours later, Mia leaned back in her chair, exhausted but satisfied with the progress they'd made. The immediate threats had been neutralized, but the fallout from the attack would require her attention for the foreseeable future. Her phone buzzed with a message from Eleanor: "Looking forward to tomorrow! See you and Sophie at the gallery? "

Mia hesitated, her fingers hovering over the keyboard. She typed out a reply, "I might have to miss this one. Huge crisis at work. I'll keep you posted." She stared at the message, reluctant to send it, knowing how much these gatherings meant to her and her friends.

Finally, she hit send, her decision made, but with a heavy heart.

The next day, as Eleanor and Sophie enjoyed the art exhibit, Mia was in her office, surrounded by monitors displaying lines of code and security logs. Her work was critical, not just to her company but to her own professional integrity. Yet, she couldn't shake off a feeling of missing out—a moment of respite with her friends, a moment to recharge.

As she debugged a line of code, her phone lit up with a photo message from Eleanor. It was a picture of Sophie standing beside a vibrant painting, both of them smiling. The text read, "We miss you! But don't worry, we're bringing the art to you"

Mia smiled, a genuine smile that eased some of the tension in her shoulders. She saved the picture, a reminder of what awaited once the storm had passed—a safe harbor in the form of her friends.

That evening, as Mia wrapped up her work, she made a promise to herself to balance her demanding career with her personal life better. She knew it wouldn't be easy, but the picture on her phone reminded her of why it was necessary. The support and understanding of Eleanor and Sophie were just as crucial to her well-being as her success in her career.

CHAPTER 8:

ARTISTIC INSPIRATIONS

S ophie's spirits were high as she walked through the bustling streets of the coastal town, heading back to her cottage after the art exhibit. The interactions with local artists and the feedback on her work had infused her with new ideas and a renewed sense of purpose. Her sketchbook was tucked under her arm, brimming with rough sketches and notes.

Upon reaching her cottage, Sophie immediately set up her workspace, the late afternoon light filtering through the windows creating a perfect setting for painting. Her latest project was inspired by her own journey of healing and the powerful landscapes of the coastal town that had become her sanctuary.

As she mixed her paints, her mind replayed the conversation she had with Eleanor about the emotive power of art. Eleanor had shared stories of how art therapy had helped many of her former students find their voice. This sparked an idea in Sophie to blend her personal experiences with a broader theme of recovery and resilience, aiming to connect with those who had similar struggles.

Sophie began with broad, sweeping strokes, laying down the deep blues and greens of the ocean. Each layer of paint added depth to the canvas, just as each day added depth to her new life. Her style was evolving, becoming more confident and expressive, a reflection of her growing inner strength.

The next morning, Sophie visited the local art supply store to pick up more canvases. The owner, Mrs. Jenkins, recognized her from the exhibit and struck up a conversation. "Your work yesterday was quite moving, Sophie. It seems you have a lot to say through your colors."

Sophie smiled, appreciating the kindness. "Thank you, Mrs. Jenkins. I'm actually planning a new series, something to hopefully help others see that there's beauty even in the tough times."

Mrs. Jenkins nodded, understandingly. "Art has a way of reaching deep, doesn't it? If you ever want to display your new series here, consider it done. We have a community wall, and your work deserves a spot."

Grateful for the offer, Sophie promised to bring in some pieces once they were ready. The support bolstered her resolve to make her art not just a personal outlet but a means of communication and healing for others.

As she worked over the next few weeks, Sophie

documented her process and shared snippets on social media. The response was overwhelmingly positive, with many expressing how much her pieces resonated with them. The engagement was not only a boost to her confidence but also solidified her desire to use her art to reach out and connect with a wider audience.

One evening, while painting a particularly challenging scene depicting a stormy sea, Sophie received a call from Eleanor. "How would you feel about showing some of your new work at the community center? They're hosting an art therapy workshop, and your pieces would be perfect to inspire discussions."

Sophie was touched and a little nervous, but she agreed. "Yes, I'd love to. It's scary, but exciting too. Maybe it's another step in my journey."

Eleanor's laughter was warm over the phone. "Exactly, dear. It's all about taking those steps, no matter how small they seem."

With each new piece, Sophie felt more connected to her community and to herself. Her art was not only a reflection of her past but a beacon for her future, guiding her and others towards healing and understanding through the power of visual storytelling.

CHAPTER 9:

UNEXPECTED FRIENDSHIP

T
he community center was abuzz with anticipation as Sophie set up her paintings for the art therapy workshop. The walls, usually bare or adorned with general community notices, now held her vibrant canvases, each one telling a story of struggle, hope, and resilience. Sophie felt a mixture of pride and vulnerability as she adjusted the lighting to best capture the depth of her colors.

Eleanor arrived early to help, bringing with her a comforting presence. She watched Sophie with admiration, seeing how much she had grown since their first meeting. "You're doing something wonderful here, Sophie," Eleanor encouraged, placing a gentle hand on her shoulder.

Sophie smiled nervously, "I hope so. I just want it to make a difference, even if it's just for one person."

As people began to filter in, Mia rushed through the door, barely on time, her face showing traces of the day's stress but also excitement to support Sophie. Seeing the paintings, Mia was struck by the emotion in each piece. "Sophie, these are incredible. You've really captured something powerful here."

The workshop began with a brief introduction by the facilitator, a local therapist specializing in expressive arts therapy. She explained how art could serve as a communication tool for those who found it difficult to express themselves verbally. "Art," she said, "allows us to say without words what we often struggle to communicate with them."

Participants were then invited to view Sophie's artwork, each piece serving as a prompt for discussion. People shared their interpretations and emotional responses, many relating deeply to the themes of transformation and healing evident in Sophie's work.

One young woman, particularly moved by a painting of a sunrise over the sea, shared her own story of overcoming grief. "This reminds me that there's always a new beginning, no matter how dark it gets," she said, tears in her eyes.

Sophie listened, her heart full, realizing her experiences and her art were touching lives, sparking conversations that might not have happened otherwise. The workshop culminated in a group activity where participants created their own pieces, inspired by the emotions and stories shared.

After the workshop, as they were cleaning up, Eleanor, Mia, and Sophie reflected on the success of the evening. "You've started something special here, Sophie," Mia said, genuinely impressed by the impact of the event.

Sophie nodded, feeling a newfound sense of purpose. "It feels right," she admitted. "Like I'm finally where I'm supposed to be."

Eleanor, observing the younger women, felt a surge of protectiveness and pride. "You both are doing remarkable things," she said. "Mia, with your groundbreaking work in tech, and Sophie, with your art that heals. I'm just happy to be a part of your journeys."

Their conversation drifted to plans for more collaborative events, perhaps involving technology and art, blending Mia and Sophie's worlds in creative ways. As they left the community center that evening, the bonds of their unexpected friendship had deepened, each woman inspired by the others' passions and commitments to making a difference in their respective fields.

CHAPTER 10:

OLD LOVE, NEW BEGINNINGS

 A fter the success of the art therapy workshop, Eleanor found herself invigorated by the energy of new endeavors and the impact they had within the community. Yet, amidst these activities, her own personal journey took an unexpected turn when she encountered a familiar face from her past.

While walking through the town's main street, Eleanor stopped to browse the window display of the local bookstore. As she peered at the latest releases, a voice from behind startled her.

"Eleanor? Eleanor Reed? Is that really you?"

Turning around, Eleanor was taken aback to see Michael Davidson, a former student from her early days of teaching. Michael had been a quiet, thoughtful young man, always with his nose in a book. Now, he stood before her, aged like herself, with streaks of gray in his hair and lines around his eyes, but still with the same gentle smile.

"Michael! I can't believe it. How many years has it been?" Eleanor asked, her voice a mixture of surprise and delight.

"Too many, Mrs. Reed. Too many," Michael chuckled. "I just moved back to town to retire and couldn't believe my luck when I saw you."

They decided to catch up over coffee, finding a quiet table at a nearby café. Michael shared stories of his years as a librarian in a bustling city, his travels, and his decision to return to his hometown for a slower pace of life. Eleanor listened intently, feeling a warm glow of pride for the life her former student had led.

As they talked, Eleanor shared her own adventures and the quieter life she'd led since retiring. She spoke of her husband's passing and how she was finding new paths and passions in her later years. The conversation flowed easily, filled with laughter and nostalgic reminiscences.

Michael's eyes shone with admiration. "You always inspired us to follow our passions, Mrs. Reed. It seems you're still living by that lesson."

The meeting ended with a promise to keep in touch, and as Eleanor walked home, she felt a spark of something she hadn't expected—a flutter of excitement at the prospect of rekindling an old connection. It was not the romantic kind, but rather an appreciation of shared history and mutual respect that had stood the test of time.

Inspired by this unexpected reunion, Eleanor began to think about other aspects of her life that might benefit from a fresh perspective. She pondered the idea of writing, perhaps starting a blog or a memoir that could weave together the rich tapestry of her experiences. The idea of sharing her insights on aging, loss, and embracing new beginnings felt increasingly appealing.

Eleanor shared her thoughts with Mia and Sophie during their next get-together. Mia, enthusiastic and supportive, offered to help set up a blog. "You have so much wisdom to share, Eleanor. Let's give it a platform," Mia suggested, her tech-savvy mind already mapping out the possibilities.

Sophie added, "And your stories could inspire your blog's visuals. I could contribute some artwork. It would be a beautiful collaboration."

Eleanor felt a surge of gratitude and excitement. What had started as a chance meeting had blossomed into an opportunity not only to reconnect with an old acquaintance but to embark on a new creative venture with her friends.

The project seemed like a perfect convergence of past and present, a way to honor her history while engaging with the present community and her newfound friends. Eleanor was ready to embrace this new chapter, filled with the joy of old love and the thrill of new beginnings.

CHAPTER 11:

MIA'S DILEMMA

 Mia sat in her sleek, glass-walled office, her eyes scanning the latest project reports on her dual monitors. The aftermath of the cyberattack had been handled well, with her team effectively mitigating the risks and restoring security. However, the constant pressure and long hours were starting to wear her down, highlighting a growing conflict between her career ambitions and her personal aspirations.

As she prepared for another video conference, her phone buzzed with a message from an unfamiliar number. Curious, Mia checked it, finding an unexpected job offer from an emerging tech startup known for its innovative approach to work-life balance and its commitment to female leadership in technology.

The message read, "Hi Mia, I'm reaching out because we've heard great things about your work at NovaTech and your advocacy for privacy in tech. We'd love to discuss a potential role for you at our company, where we believe your skills and vision would be invaluable. Plus, we're committed to ensuring our team members have the time they need for personal development and fulfillment outside of work."

Mia stared at the message, her heart racing with both excitement and uncertainty. The offer was tempting, especially the promise of a better balance between her professional responsibilities and her personal life. It could give her the space she needed to revive her blog, spend more time with friends, and possibly even start a relationship.

Later that day, she met with Eleanor and Sophie at their favorite café to seek their advice. After explaining the situation and reading out the job offer, Mia looked at her friends, her expression torn.

Eleanor, ever the wise advisor, sipped her tea thoughtfully. "It sounds like a wonderful opportunity, Mia. But it's also a big change. Think about what you truly value and what makes you happiest in the long run."

Sophie chimed in, her voice encouraging. "Mia, you've been amazing at your job, but I've also seen how much you've sacrificed. Maybe this new place could be where you find a better balance. Plus, you'd be paving the way for more women in tech leadership, which is awesome!"

Mia nodded, grateful for their insights. The decision wasn't easy. She was deeply invested in her current projects at NovaTech, and she feared that leaving might disrupt the progress she had helped to drive. However, the new role offered not just another job, but a lifestyle change—one that could bring her closer to the life she envisioned for herself.

After the meeting, Mia walked along the beach,

letting the sound of the waves help her ponder her decision. She thought about her long days, her missed social events, and the personal projects she had put on hold. Then, she thought about the possibility of change, of a new environment that valued her well-being as much as her skills.

As the sun set, casting a warm glow over the sea, Mia made her decision. She would take the interview and explore the opportunity. If the new company was as promising as it seemed, it might be the fresh start she needed to achieve the balance she longed for.

Returning home, Mia crafted her response to the job offer, her fingers steady as she typed. She was ready to explore this new path, hopeful that it would lead to a brighter, more balanced future.

CHAPTER 12:

ART SHOW SUCCESS

S ophie's recent works, infused with her personal journey and the emotional landscapes of the seaside town, were now ready for her first solo art show. The local art community and her newfound friends, Eleanor and Mia, had played crucial roles in bringing this event to life. The anticipation had built over weeks of preparation, and today, the quaint local gallery was abuzz with visitors eager to view Sophie's expressions on canvas.

The gallery was filled with soft lighting that highlighted the vibrant colors and bold textures of her paintings. Each piece told a story—of struggle, of resilience, of the triumphant beauty in overcoming. Sophie walked among the guests, her nervousness balanced by the pride she felt in her work. As she explained her inspirations and techniques, the feedback was overwhelmingly positive, with several attendees expressing deep connections to her themes.

Eleanor, ever supportive, mingled with the crowd, overhearing the praises and seeing the impact of Sophie's art. "You've done something wonderful here, Sophie," she said, her voice thick with emotion. "You're not just creating art; you're touching lives, healing wounds."

Mia, despite the looming decision about her job offer, had made it a point to be there. She watched Sophie from across the room, impressed by her poise and the way her art resonated with the audience. "I knew she was talented, but seeing all this... Sophie's really made a huge leap," Mia commented to Eleanor as they shared a moment away from the crowd.

During the show, a local art critic, who had been observing quietly, approached Sophie. "Your work is compelling. It speaks of truth and pain, yet there's a hopeful undertone that's quite rare," he noted, his keen eyes scanning the canvases. "I'd like to write a feature on your journey and your art. Would you be open to that?"

Sophie's heart skipped a beat. This was more than she had hoped for. "Yes, absolutely, I would love that," she replied, her voice steady despite the excitement bubbling inside her.

As the evening drew to a close, several pieces had sold, and Sophie had received numerous invitations to showcase her work at other venues and events. It was more than a successful show; it was the beginning of a promising career in the arts.

After the guests had left and the gallery was quiet, Sophie, Eleanor, and Mia sat among the remaining pieces, sharing a bottle of wine. "Tonight was incredible," Sophie said, a glow of satisfaction in her eyes. "Thank you both for being here, for everything."

Eleanor raised her glass. "To Sophie's success, and to all the future successes I have no doubt are coming your way."

Mia joined in, her thoughts momentarily away from her own dilemmas. "Here's to new beginnings—

Sophie's, mine, all of ours."

The night ended with a sense of completion, but also a promise of new beginnings. For Sophie, the art show had not only marked a significant milestone in her artistic journey but also reaffirmed her belief in her path and the community she had found.

CHAPTER 13:

THE DECISION

Mia sat in the minimalist lounge area of the startup's headquarters, her mind racing as she awaited her final interview. The building itself was a testament to the company's commitment to innovation, with open workspaces, green walls, and an abundance of natural light. Yet, even in this inspiring environment, Mia's thoughts were tumultuous, weighed down by the gravity of her decision.

Her interviews so far had been promising. The team was dynamic and forward-thinking, and the role they proposed aligned perfectly with her aspirations to lead without sacrificing her personal life. They discussed flexible hours, remote work options, and a strong emphasis on team well-being—practices that NovaTech was only slowly beginning to consider.

As she was called into the conference room for her final discussion, Mia took a deep breath, steadying herself. The company's CEO, a woman known for her visionary leadership in tech, greeted Mia with a warm smile.

"Mia, I've been looking forward to our chat," the CEO began, her tone both friendly and professional. "Your experience at NovaTech is impressive, but it's your passion for ethical tech that really drew us to you. We think you could be a key player in driving our company forward."

Mia listened, her excitement growing with each word. This was exactly the type of leadership role she had been craving—one where she could influence company culture and policy, not just manage projects.

"We're ready to offer you the position, Mia," the CEO continued. "We believe you can help us make a real difference in the industry. What do you think?"

Mia paused, considering her options. The offer was everything she had hoped for, yet the thought of leaving her team at NovaTech, where she had built her career, was daunting. But as she thought about her recent exhaustion and the constant struggle to balance her work with her personal life, the choice became clear.

"I'm honored, and I accept," Mia replied, a mix of relief and anticipation in her voice. "I'm excited to be a part of your team and contribute to something I truly believe in."

The CEO's smile widened. "Welcome aboard, Mia. We're thrilled to have you."

Leaving the building, Mia felt a weight lift off her shoulders. She had made the decision based on her values and her needs, not out of fear or habit. As she drove home, she phoned Eleanor and Sophie to share the news.

Eleanor was overjoyed. "Mia, that's wonderful! I knew you'd make the right choice for yourself. When do you start?"

"In two weeks," Mia replied, her voice brimming with enthusiasm. "I'll have some time to transition my projects and say proper goodbyes at NovaTech."

Sophie's voice was equally supportive. "Congrats, Mia! It sounds like a perfect fit for you. Let's celebrate soon!"

With her friends' congratulations ringing in her ears, Mia felt reassured in her decision. She was stepping into a new phase of her life, one that promised not just professional fulfillment but personal happiness as well.

CHAPTER 14:

ART IN THE PARK

S ophie's recent art show success had sparked an idea in her mind—an outdoor art event that would engage the entire community and provide a platform for local artists to showcase their talents. With the help of Eleanor and Mia, who were now well-versed in organizing and promoting events, Sophie began planning "Art in the Park," an event set in the local public gardens.

As the day of the event approached, the gardens were transformed. Canvases were hung from trees, sculptures placed amongst the flowerbeds, and interactive art installations invited onlookers to participate. Local musicians and food vendors added to the festival atmosphere, creating a vibrant, creative space that drew a crowd from across the town.

Eleanor took on the role of coordinating volunteers, her experience in managing school events proving invaluable. She moved through the park with a clipboard, ensuring that each artist had what they needed and that the event ran smoothly. Her blog had featured several posts about the upcoming event, which had helped to generate buzz and attract a large turnout.

Mia, ever the tech enthusiast, had set up a digital registration booth for visitors, where they could sign up for newsletters and future workshops. Her new job's flexible hours allowed her to dedicate time to support Sophie's initiative, and she found the community engagement deeply fulfilling.

As people wandered through the park, stopping to admire the artwork or to participate in a painting workshop, Sophie felt a surge of pride. Her journey from a fearful newcomer to a community influencer was evident in how confidently she interacted with the attendees, discussing her art and encouraging young artists.

One particular piece, a large canvas depicting the seaside at dawn, became the centerpiece of the event. It caught the eye of the local mayor, who stopped to chat with Sophie. "This is a wonderful addition to our community events calendar," he remarked, clearly impressed. "It's initiatives like these that enrich our town."

Sophie smiled, her heart swelling with the acknowledgment. "Thank you, Mayor. It's my way of giving back to the community that has welcomed me so warmly."

As the event drew to a close, Eleanor, Mia, and Sophie gathered to reflect on the day. "This was a fantastic turnout," Mia observed, her eyes scanning the content crowd. "It looks like 'Art in the Park' might become an annual thing."

"I hope so," Sophie replied. "It's been amazing to see how art can bring people together, to share and celebrate."

Eleanor nodded, her eyes twinkling with pride. "You've done something special today, Sophie. We all have. It's a testament to the power of community and creativity."

As they helped pack up the remaining artworks and installations, the women felt a shared sense of accomplishment. They had not only brought art to the park but had woven it into the fabric of their community, creating a tapestry of culture, connection, and support.

CHAPTER 15:

A HEALTH SCARE

 few weeks after the successful "Art in the Park" event, Eleanor was faced with a personal challenge that tested her resilience. It began one morning when she felt an unusual dizziness and a sharp pain in her chest. Initially dismissing it as fatigue from her recent activities, she soon realized it was something more serious when the symptoms persisted.

Reluctantly, Eleanor decided to visit her doctor, who recommended immediate tests to rule out any cardiac issues. The waiting and uncertainty that followed were grueling for Eleanor, who had always been the pillar of strength in her circle.

Sophie and Mia rallied around her, offering support and companionship. Mia, adapting to her new job's flexibility, was able to accompany Eleanor to some of her appointments, while Sophie used her visits to bring meals and keep Eleanor's spirits up with light conversation and updates about the art community.

The day of the diagnosis was tense. Sitting in the doctor's office, Eleanor held Mia's hand tightly. The doctor entered with her results, her expression a professional blend of empathy and reassurance. "Eleanor, you've had a minor heart attack, but fortunately, we caught it early. You're going to need medication and some lifestyle changes, but I expect a full recovery."

The relief was palpable, but so was the shock. Eleanor, who had always taken her health for granted, now faced the reality of her vulnerability. The drive home was quiet, each woman lost in her thoughts.

Back at Eleanor's house, the three friends gathered in the living room, a space that had witnessed many of their shared confidences and plans. Eleanor, ever the hostess despite the day's events, served tea, her hands slightly trembling.

"Mia, Sophie, I can't thank you enough for being here," Eleanor started, her voice steady but softer than usual. "Today was a wake-up call. I need to slow down, focus on my health."

Sophie, moved by Eleanor's openness, replied gently, "We're here for you, Eleanor. Just like you've been here for us. Maybe this is a chance to explore those parts of life you've been putting off—more of your writing, maybe some travel once you're feeling stronger."

Mia nodded, her analytical mind already considering practical adjustments. "And we can help manage some of the community projects you've been overseeing. Don't worry about 'Art in the Park' or any other events. Sophie and I can handle things for a while."

Eleanor smiled, her eyes glistening with unshed tears. "I'm lucky to have you both. I guess it's time I took my own advice about embracing new beginnings, isn't it?"

The conversation shifted to planning Eleanor's recovery and adjustments to her daily routines.

Plans were made for healthier meal prep, gentle exercise routines, and perhaps most importantly, more regular, relaxed gatherings just like this one.

As they continued talking late into the evening, the initial fear and uncertainty transformed into a collective determination. Eleanor's health scare, while frightening, had brought them even closer, deepening the bonds of their friendship and underscoring the importance of health and well-being in their busy lives.

CHAPTER 16:

THE BREAKTHROUGH

Mia had been at her new job for a few weeks now, and the transition had been as challenging as it was exhilarating. The startup's culture was refreshingly open and innovative, but the expectations were high, and Mia found herself at the center of a critical project that could define her early tenure with the company.

The project involved developing a new privacy-centric feature for the company's main product, a task that aligned perfectly with Mia's passions and expertise. However, the technical challenges were formidable, and the team had hit several roadblocks that threatened to derail their timeline.

Determined to make her mark, Mia dove headfirst into the problem. She spent long hours collaborating with her team, testing new approaches, and refining their code. The breakthrough came one late evening when, after numerous failed attempts, Mia and her team finally found a solution that was both elegant and effective.

"We did it!" she exclaimed, hardly believing the results on her screen. The team erupted in cheers, their previous frustrations giving way to a sense of accomplishment and relief.

Flushed with success, Mia sent an excited text to Eleanor and Sophie: "Big breakthrough at work today! Can't wait to tell you both about it. Dinner soon?"

Their responses came quickly, full of congratulations and eagerness to celebrate her success. Plans were made for a dinner at their favorite local restaurant, a spot that had become their go-to for celebrating personal victories and supporting each other through challenges.

At dinner, Mia detailed the technical intricacies and strategic thinking behind their success. Eleanor listened with pride, marveling at Mia's ability to take charge and innovate under pressure. Sophie, always inspired by her friends' achievements, proposed a toast.

"To Mia, who reminds us that perseverance and passion can turn challenges into triumphs," Sophie said, raising her glass.

Eleanor chimed in, "And to all of us, for finding strength in our friendship and inspiration in each other's journeys."

The conversation then turned to more personal updates. Eleanor shared about her recovery and how she was gradually incorporating more activity into her routine, following her doctor's advice. She spoke about her plans to start a new series on her blog, focusing on healthy living and heart disease awareness, inspired by her recent scare.

Sophie talked about a new series of paintings she had started, motivated by the community's response to "Art in the Park." Her work was evolving, becoming more abstract and introspective, reflecting her growing confidence and artistic vision.

As the evening wound down, the three women felt a renewed sense of connection and purpose. They had each faced their own challenges, but together, they had found a way to thrive, drawing strength from their friendship and their individual passions.

Walking home under the starlit sky, Mia felt

incredibly fortunate. Her new job was proving to be everything she had hoped for, and her friends were thriving alongside her. The challenges of the past few weeks had tested her, but they had also shown her what she was capable of achieving with the right support and determination.

CHAPTER 17:

NEW LOVE, NEW BEGINNINGS

E leanor's journey through recovery had been a time of reflection and adaptation. Encouraged by her friends and motivated by her recent health scare, she had begun blogging more frequently about her experiences, focusing on healthy aging and emotional wellness. Her audience was growing, and with it, a new sense of purpose blossomed within her.

During one of her morning walks—a new routine she'd adopted since her health scare—Eleanor ran into Michael, the former student she had reconnected with several weeks earlier. Their chance meetings had become more frequent, and Eleanor found herself looking forward to their conversations more than she had expected.

This morning, Michael had a different air about

him as he approached Eleanor on the walking trail. "Eleanor, I've been thinking a lot about our conversations, about how inspiring I find your approach to life," he started, a hint of nervousness in his voice. "I wonder if you might like to join me for dinner this weekend? There's a new restaurant in town I think you'd enjoy."

Eleanor, surprised by the invitation but pleased, felt a warm flush of excitement. "I'd like that, Michael. It sounds lovely," she responded, her smile genuine and wide.

As Saturday evening arrived, Eleanor dressed with care, choosing a soft lavender blouse that complimented her eyes, a detail she hadn't paid attention to in quite some time. Michael picked her up, and they drove to the restaurant, a cozy place with a view of the ocean.

Dinner was a delightful affair, filled with shared memories of the past and discussions about their aspirations. Michael spoke passionately about his love for literature and his volunteer work at the local library, while Eleanor shared her blogging adventures and the fulfillment it brought her.

As the evening drew to a close, Michael reached across the table, his hand lightly covering Eleanor's. "I'm really glad we did this," he said, his eyes earnest. "I've come to look forward to our talks, Eleanor. There's a connection here I can't quite put into words."

Eleanor felt the same, a connection that was both comforting and exhilarating. "I feel it too, Michael. It's nice to discover someone who shares similar passions, at this point in our lives," she admitted, her voice soft but clear.

Their dinner dates became a regular occurrence, and over time, Eleanor found herself opening up more to Michael, enjoying the companionship and the new romantic feelings that were blossoming. She blogged about her experiences, though keeping some details private, her posts resonating with many who were also navigating the complexities of dating later in life.

Meanwhile, Mia and Sophie were delighted to see Eleanor so happy. They supported her wholeheartedly, curious about every little detail and eager to offer advice when asked. The three friends continued to meet regularly, their conversations enriched by Eleanor's newfound experiences in love.

As Eleanor embraced this new chapter, she found that love, much like life, could offer new beginnings at any age. Her heart, both figuratively and literally stronger now, was open to the possibilities that lay ahead.

CHAPTER 18:

MIA'S COMMITMENT

M ia had settled into her new role with a dynamism that impressed both her colleagues and herself. Her work on privacy-centric features had gained traction, and she was now spearheading a major project that aimed to revolutionize user data protection. The success of her initial efforts had not only validated her decision to switch jobs but had also energized her with a purpose she hadn't felt in years.

Despite her professional accomplishments, Mia found herself grappling with the personal side of her life. Her commitment to her career had always come at the expense of her personal relationships, a trade-off that was becoming increasingly unsatisfactory. Inspired by Eleanor's newfound romance and Sophie's growing connection with the community through her art, Mia began to reassess her own life choices.

During a late evening at the office, Mia found herself working alone, the quiet a stark contrast to the usual daytime bustle. Her thoughts drifted to her recent conversations with Eleanor and Sophie about balance and fulfillment. It was then that she decided it was time to make a change—not in her career, but in her personal life.

Mia started by revisiting old hobbies that she had set aside. She joined a local cycling club, something she had always enjoyed but never made time for. It was during these weekend rides that she met Alex, a fellow tech enthusiast with a penchant for outdoor adventures. Their shared interests quickly led to deeper conversations, and Mia found herself drawn to Alex's easygoing nature and insightful perspectives.

Their relationship progressed naturally, and Mia found that dating Alex did not require her to compromise on her professional ambitions. Instead, it complemented her life, adding a layer of personal happiness that enhanced her overall wellbeing.

Encouraged by this new development, Mia shared her experiences with Eleanor and Sophie during one of their regular meet-ups. "It's different this time," Mia explained, her voice reflecting a mixture of surprise and contentment. "I've realized that I don't have to choose between a fulfilling career and a fulfilling personal life. It's possible to have both, as long as I make the commitment."

Eleanor nodded, her eyes twinkling with approval. "It's all about finding the right balance, Mia. I'm so happy you've found someone who respects and shares your passions."

Sophie chimed in, her tone playful yet sincere, "We need to meet this Alex soon, Mia! He sounds like a keeper."

As the evening drew to a close, Mia felt a profound sense of gratitude for the support of her friends and the new direction her life was taking. The challenges of balancing her commitments remained, but with a supportive partner and a clearer understanding of her own needs, Mia was more confident than ever in her ability to manage them.

With new relationships blossoming and each woman navigating her own path towards fulfillment, the trio's bond continued to strengthen, providing a solid foundation of support and understanding as they each ventured into new and promising chapters of their lives.

CHAPTER 19:

SOPHIE'S NATIONAL EXHIBITION

S ophie's local success with her art had started to ripple outward, catching the attention of national art circles. Her vivid, emotionally resonant paintings had struck a chord with a broader audience, leading to an invitation to showcase her work at a prestigious national exhibition. This was a milestone Sophie had dreamed of, and now it was becoming a reality.

As she prepared for the exhibition, Sophie felt a blend of excitement and nervousness. Her new series, which delved into themes of transformation and resilience, was more personal and abstract than her previous work. It was a risk, but one that she felt compelled to take, driven by her own experiences and the encouragement of her friends.

Eleanor and Mia were instrumental in helping her prepare. Eleanor, with her newfound enthusiasm for blogging, wrote a feature piece on Sophie's journey and upcoming exhibition, which brought even more attention to Sophie's work. Mia, ever the tech-savvy friend, helped set up an online gallery, allowing Sophie's work to reach potential buyers and art enthusiasts worldwide.

The night before the exhibition, the three women gathered in Sophie's studio, surrounded by the canvases that would soon be displayed. They toasted to Sophie's success and the adventures ahead. Eleanor shared words of encouragement, reminding Sophie of how far she had come. "Remember, each piece tells a story that only you can tell. Be proud of that," Eleanor said, her voice warm with pride.

Mia added, "And you're not just showing your art; you're showing your heart. People will see that, and they'll connect with it. You've got this."

The exhibition itself was held in a large, airy gallery in a major city, attended by critics, collectors, and art lovers from across the country. As guests moved through the space, Sophie's work received widespread acclaim for its depth and boldness. The critics praised her unique ability to convey complex emotions through color and form, and several pieces sold before the exhibition even concluded.

One particularly poignant piece, a large canvas depicting a storm breaking over a calm sea, was the highlight of the show. It symbolized the tumultuous yet hopeful journey not just of the artist but of anyone who had ever faced and overcome adversity.

After the exhibition, Sophie's reputation as a rising artist was solidified. Offers to exhibit in other galleries and to participate in international art fairs came flooding in, opening doors to new opportunities and challenges.

Reflecting on the whirlwind of her success, Sophie felt a profound gratitude for her friends, whose unwavering support had helped her reach this point. "I couldn't have done any of this without you both," she told Eleanor and Mia during a celebratory dinner. "You helped me believe in my art and myself."

The success of the national exhibition was not just a personal victory for Sophie but a testament to the strength of their friendship, which had become a foundational support system for each of them. As they looked forward to the future, each woman knew that no matter what challenges or successes lay ahead, their bond would remain a source of strength and inspiration.

CHAPTER 20:

HEARTFELT GOODBYES

fter the exhilarating success of Sophie's national exhibition, the trio found themselves navigating new phases in their lives with renewed vigor and confidence. Eleanor, inspired by her relationship with Michael and her continuous blogging success, decided it was time for another significant life change. She announced to Mia and Sophie that she planned to move into a senior living community—a decision that, while difficult, promised new friendships and activities suited to her lifestyle.

Eleanor had always been the cornerstone of their

group, providing wisdom and stability. Her decision brought mixed feelings for Mia and Sophie, who had come to rely on her steady presence. However, they both understood the importance of her finding a community where she could continue to thrive and explore new interests.

The move was planned for the end of the month, which gave them a few weeks to prepare. Mia and Sophie supported Eleanor in downsizing her belongings, a task that brought about nostalgic moments and heartfelt discussions. They sifted through years of memorabilia, each item holding stories and memories.

During one of these packing sessions, Eleanor found an old photo album filled with pictures of her teaching days, her early years with her late husband, and various life milestones. Sharing these memories with Mia and Sophie, she realized how much her life had impacted others and how her new blog had allowed her to continue that influence.

"Look at all these lives intertwined with mine. I'm ready to make new memories, but I'll carry these old ones close to my heart," Eleanor said, a sentimental smile playing on her lips as she carefully placed the album in a box labeled 'Keep.'

As the moving day approached, Mia organized a farewell party to celebrate Eleanor's new journey. Friends from various stages of Eleanor's life gathered, along with people she had touched through her community work and blog. The party was bittersweet, filled with laughter and tears, as everyone shared how Eleanor had influenced their lives.

Sophie presented Eleanor with a special gift—a custom painting of the seaside town, capturing the place where their friendships had flourished. "So you can always remember the times we shared here, no matter where you are," Sophie said, her voice thick with emotion.

Eleanor was deeply moved, holding the painting close. "I will treasure this, and all the moments we've shared. Remember, this isn't goodbye. It's just a new chapter," she reassured them, her eyes shining with tears.

The day Eleanor moved, Mia and Sophie helped her settle into her new apartment, hanging her favorite paintings and arranging her things just so. As they said their goodbyes, Eleanor hugged each of them tightly. "You both have given me so much joy. Let's promise to visit often and keep sharing our journeys, no matter where we are."

Driving back from the senior living community, Mia and Sophie felt a sense of emptiness but also gratitude for the time they had spent with Eleanor and the growth they had experienced together. They knew that while the dynamics of their meetings might change, the bond they shared would endure, continually enriched by new experiences and shared memories.

CHAPTER 21:

A NEW PROJECT

s Eleanor settled into her new community, embracing the opportunities and friendships it offered, Mia and Sophie found themselves at a crossroads, each considering how to move forward in their own lives while maintaining the bond they shared with Eleanor and each other.

Mia, feeling inspired by her recent professional successes and the personal growth she experienced from her relationship with Alex, proposed a new project to Sophie. She suggested they collaborate on a tech-art installation that would combine their skills—Sophie's artistry and her own technological expertise—to create an interactive experience that explored themes of connection and innovation.

Sophie was immediately intrigued by the idea. Her recent experiences had opened her up to exploring new forms of artistic expression, and the concept of integrating technology with her art was both challenging and exciting.

They began brainstorming sessions, during which Mia introduced Sophie to various interactive technologies, such as augmented reality (AR) and motion sensors, that could bring a dynamic element to her paintings. Sophie, in turn, proposed ways her art could be transformed into an immersive experience, allowing viewers to engage with it on multiple sensory levels.

Their project, titled "Connected Realms," aimed to create an installation where art and technology would interact dynamically with the audience, changing and responding to their presence and actions. This idea symbolized their belief in the power of connection—between individuals, disciplines, and communities.

As they developed the project, Mia and Sophie frequently visited Eleanor to seek her insights and keep her involved in their creative process. Eleanor, thriving in her new environment, provided valuable feedback and moral support, proud to see her friends taking such innovative steps forward.

The development phase brought its challenges— technical hurdles, conceptual refinements, and logistical issues—but Mia and Sophie tackled each obstacle with a combination of creativity and determination. They also decided to document their process in a blog, which they hoped would inspire others to explore interdisciplinary collaborations.

Months later, "Connected Realms" was ready to be unveiled at a local art and technology festival. The installation featured large-scale projections of Sophie's artworks, which transformed in real-time according to audience interactions captured through sensors. Mia had programmed the system to not only respond to movement but also to adapt to the collective mood of the viewers, using AI to interpret emotional cues and modify the visual experience accordingly.

The festival was a huge success. Attendees were captivated by the installation, often lingering to discuss the technology and the art, marveling at how seamlessly they blended to create something entirely new and impactful. The feedback was overwhelmingly positive, with many expressing appreciation for the thought-provoking way the project bridged the gap between art and technology.

Following the festival, Mia and Sophie were invited to showcase "Connected Realms" at other events and venues, both nationally and internationally. The project not only enhanced their professional reputations but also deepened their friendship, proving that their collaborative spirit could lead to remarkable achievements.

Eleanor, attending one of the exhibitions, stood back with a proud smile, watching the diverse crowds interact with the installation. "You've both done something wonderful here," she told Mia and Sophie, her eyes reflecting the dynamic lights of the installation. "You've connected more than just realms of art and technology; you've connected hearts and minds."

CHAPTER 22:

REFLECTIONS BY THE SEA

fter the success of "Connected Realms," Mia and Sophie decided to take a brief respite to reflect on their achievements and plan their next steps. They chose a weekend retreat at a small coastal cabin, a place close to where their friendship had blossomed and where they had shared many pivotal moments with Eleanor.

As they arrived, the familiar scent of salt and seaweed welcomed them, a reminder of past introspections and decisions made along this very shore. The cabin, nestled among windswept dunes, offered a panoramic view of the ocean, its rhythmical waves a perfect backdrop for deep conversations and creative brainstorming.

The first evening, as they watched the sunset paint the sky in shades of orange and pink, Mia and Sophie discussed how far they had come. Mia shared her thoughts on the potential expansion of their project, envisioning a series of installations across different cities, each tailored to reflect local cultures and artistic expressions.

Sophie, inspired by the changing tides, mused about integrating natural elements into her art, perhaps starting a new series that explored the environmental impacts of technology. "There's something about this place that always brings new ideas," Sophie remarked, her eyes reflecting the last of the sunset's glow.

The next morning, they took a long walk along the beach, the cool water lapping at their feet. Conversation turned to Eleanor, who was thriving in her new community but missed their regular in-person gatherings. They planned a surprise visit for her upcoming birthday, wanting to show her that despite the physical distance, their friendship remained a constant in their lives.

As they gathered driftwood and shells along the shore, Mia proposed another collaborative project, this time involving community-based art and technology workshops that could bridge generational gaps. "Imagine combining Eleanor's educational expertise, your artistic vision, and my tech background," Mia suggested enthusiastically.

Sophie loved the idea, seeing it as a way to give back to the community and to engage with different age groups, potentially bringing art and technology to schools and senior centers.

Their weekend by the sea concluded with a pledge to pursue this new project, feeling recharged by the ocean's vastness and the solitude that had allowed them to reconnect with their core motivations.

Returning to their respective homes, Mia and Sophie felt a renewed sense of purpose. They reached out to Eleanor to discuss their idea, and she was immediately on board, excited to contribute and to integrate her own experiences and insights.

The project quickly took shape, dubbed "Generational Bridges." It started locally but soon gained traction, receiving interest from educational institutions and community centers eager to participate. Mia, Sophie, and Eleanor found themselves once again at the forefront of an innovative venture, each bringing their unique strengths to ensure its success.

As "Generational Bridges" launched, the trio stood together at a community event, watching children and seniors interact with an installation that combined Sophie's art with interactive tech elements designed by Mia. Eleanor facilitated discussions and activities that bridged understanding and curiosity across ages.

Their continued collaboration was not just a testament to their friendship but also a reflection of their shared commitment to making a meaningful impact. Each woman knew that whatever the future held, their collective efforts and individual passions would keep them bonded, driving them to explore new horizons together.

CHAPTER 23:

REFLECTIONS

 A s "Generational Bridges" grew from concept to community staple, Mia, Sophie, and Eleanor found moments to pause and reflect on the individual and collective journeys that had brought them here. Each woman had faced her own challenges and triumphs, yet their shared endeavors continued to weave a rich tapestry of friendship and purpose.

Mia was thriving in her role at the tech startup, now a leading figure in advocating for ethical technology practices. Her balance of work and personal life had become a model for her colleagues, and her relationship with Alex had deepened, grounded in mutual respect and shared passions. Yet, she was contemplating a more ambitious step—starting her own company to implement the ethical practices she championed, potentially changing the tech landscape dramatically.

Sophie's artistic reputation had solidified with each exhibition, and her work was now recognized nationally. The integration of environmental themes into her art had sparked a new movement among artists and activists alike, leading to collaborative projects that spanned the globe. But for Sophie, the pull to expand her horizons was strong; she considered a sabbatical to travel and draw inspiration from different cultures, aiming to bring a more global perspective to her work.

Eleanor, comfortably settled into her new community, had become a beloved figure among her peers. Her blog was now a well-regarded resource for those navigating the complexities of aging with grace. With Michael by her side, she had found a late-life romance that was both enriching and supportive. Yet, Eleanor felt a drive to compile her experiences and lessons into a book, hoping to leave a legacy that could inspire generations to come.

As autumn turned to winter, the trio planned a reunion at their favorite coastal retreat, where they had spent many reflective moments together. It was a chance to share their thoughts, dreams, and potential plans for the future.

Sitting by the fireplace, watching the flames dance and crackle, they each took turns outlining their hopes and uncertainties.

Mia shared her idea of starting a new venture, seeking advice and encouragement. Sophie and Eleanor listened intently, offering their insights and reassuring Mia of her strength and capabilities. "You have always been a pioneer, Mia," Sophie said. "This new path seems like a natural evolution for you."

Sophie explained her desire to travel and study art from different cultures, eager to expand her creative boundaries. "I feel like there's so much more to learn and explore," she expressed, her eyes alight with excitement. Eleanor and Mia supported her decision, promising to keep the home fires burning in her absence.

Eleanor discussed her book project, outlining the chapters and the themes she wished to cover. "I want this book to be a beacon for those walking a similar path," she stated, her voice filled with conviction. Mia and Sophie offered to help with research and editing, making it a collaborative effort.

As they talked late into the night, the bonds of their friendship deepened further, each woman grateful for the others' presence in her life. They had become more than friends; they were each other's champions, confidants, and collaborators.

The weekend ended with promises to support each other's ambitions and to reunite regularly, no matter where their individual journeys took them. As they hugged goodbye, they knew that their connection would endure, sustained by mutual respect, love, and the unbreakable threads of shared experiences.

CHAPTER 24:

MIA'S NEW VENTURE

Mia's decision to start her own tech company was not taken lightly. It was born out of years of experience and a deep-seated desire to influence the tech industry more profoundly. Her vision was to create a company that not only excelled in innovative technology but also upheld the highest standards of ethics and transparency, making it a leader in responsible tech development.

After their weekend of reflections by the sea, Mia began putting her plans into action. She spent weeks meticulously drafting her business plan, focusing on a platform that would use artificial intelligence to enhance data privacy rather than exploit it. Her goal was to create software that could be used by other businesses to protect their customers' data, ensuring privacy by design.

Eleanor and Sophie, ever supportive, provided feedback and encouragement through video chats and emails as Mia navigated the complexities of entrepreneurship. Alex, who had experience in startup environments, helped refine her pitch to potential investors, emphasizing the unique selling points of Mia's business model.

The search for the right investors was challenging. Mia attended numerous networking events and pitch meetings, facing skepticism and enthusiasm in equal measure. Her resolve was tested repeatedly, but her clarity of purpose and the solid foundation of her business plan eventually won over a group of investors who were committed to ethical business practices.

With funding secured, Mia set up her office in a vibrant tech hub in the city. She was deliberate in creating a workspace that reflected her company's values, with open workspaces, plenty of green plants, and art pieces commissioned from Sophie to inspire creativity and remind her team of the beauty in ethical work.

Hiring the right team was Mia's next big challenge. She sought individuals who were not only tech-savvy but also shared her vision of a more ethical tech industry. Each candidate went through a rigorous interview process, ensuring they were a fit for the company's culture and long-term goals.

As the team came together, Mia focused on developing her platform. The initial months were a whirlwind of activity, with coding marathons, strategy sessions, and continuous testing. The pressure was immense, but Mia thrived under it, driven by the knowledge that her work could change the industry for the better.

Finally, the platform was ready for launch. The launch event was a carefully orchestrated affair attended by tech industry leaders, journalists, and influencers in the ethical tech space. Mia presented her product with confidence, showcasing its capabilities and the philosophy behind it.

The reception was overwhelmingly positive. The platform was praised for its innovative approach to privacy and data security, and Mia's company quickly gained clients eager to integrate her technology into their operations.

In the months that followed, Mia's company grew

rapidly, expanding its client base and receiving accolades for its commitment to changing the tech landscape. Mia, however, remained grounded, often reflecting on the weekend by the sea that had solidified her resolve.

Her regular updates to Eleanor and Sophie, filled with challenges and triumphs, were a testament to their enduring friendship and mutual support. Despite their different paths, their bond remained a constant source of strength and inspiration.

CHAPTER 25:

SOPHIE'S ARTISTIC JOURNEY ABROAD

S ophie had always been intrigued by the idea of exploring the world, believing that every culture could offer new insights and inspirations for her art. With her friend Mia successfully launching her tech company and Eleanor deeply engaged in writing her book, Sophie felt it was the perfect time to embark on her sabbatical, a journey to explore and study different art forms around the globe.

She began her travels in Europe, drawn to its rich artistic heritage. Her first stop was Paris, where she immersed herself in the masterpieces housed in the

Louvre and the Musée d'Orsay. Walking the same streets that artists like Monet and Picasso once did, Sophie felt a deep connection to the city's historical reverence for art.

In Paris, Sophie attended workshops on impressionist techniques, which influenced her own style, adding a new layer of depth and emotion to her work. She began a series of sketches and small paintings, capturing the essence of Parisian life—its bustling cafés, serene gardens, and vibrant street scenes.

Her journey then took her to Venice during the Biennale, an international art exhibition that provided her with the opportunity to engage with contemporary artists from around the world. The innovative use of media and the powerful themes explored in the Biennale artworks inspired Sophie to experiment with new materials and concepts, pushing her creative boundaries.

In Venice, she experimented with combining traditional painting techniques with digital elements, inspired by the work she had done with Mia. This led to a small exhibition in a local gallery, where her pieces, blending the old and new, were well-received, garnering attention from international art critics and collectors.

Sophie documented her travels and artistic experiments on a blog, which quickly gained a following among art enthusiasts and fellow travelers. Her posts were not just about art but also about the personal transformation she experienced as she delved deeper into different cultures and their unique expressions of beauty and meaning.

After Europe, Sophie traveled to Japan, where she studied traditional Japanese art forms like ink painting and woodblock printing. The simplicity and discipline of these techniques taught her new ways to approach space and detail in her work, influencing her subsequent pieces, which embodied a blend of minimalism and intricate detail.

Throughout her travels, Sophie kept in close contact with Mia and Eleanor, sharing her experiences and the new art techniques she was exploring. They continued to support each other virtually, celebrating each new success and offering advice during challenges.

As her sabbatical year drew to a close, Sophie felt transformed, not just as an artist but as a person. Her journey had enriched her understanding of the world and deepened her appreciation for the diversity of human expression.

Returning home, Sophie organized an exhibition titled "Journeys in Art," featuring the works she had created abroad. The exhibition was a resounding success, with pieces selling out and excellent reviews in art journals. Her journey had not only expanded her artistic horizons but also established her as a prominent figure in the international art community.

Reunited with Mia and Eleanor, Sophie shared her plans to continue exploring art's role in cultural exchange and communication, eager to start her next projects with a renewed sense of purpose and inspiration.

CHAPTER 26:

ELEANOR'S LEGACY

Eleanor's journey into the world of writing had been as therapeutic as it had been enlightening. Inspired by her own life experiences and the profound discussions with her closest friends, Mia and Sophie, Eleanor had dedicated herself to writing a book that encapsulated her philosophies on aging, friendship, and living a meaningful life.

The process of writing the book, tentatively titled "Seasons of Wisdom," had been both challenging and rewarding. Eleanor meticulously wove together personal anecdotes, insights from her blogging experience, and lessons learned from her late-life adventures, including her move to the senior living community and her rejuvenating romance with

Michael.

As she neared the completion of her manuscript, Eleanor organized a small gathering at her home with Mia and Sophie. She wanted to share the first draft of her book with them, seeking their feedback as they had been integral to her narrative, not just as characters in her story but as critical influences on her thoughts and decisions.

The evening was warm and filled with anticipation as Eleanor read excerpts from her manuscript. Her voice, steady and clear, brought the words to life, painting vivid pictures of their shared experiences and her reflections on them.

Mia and Sophie listened intently, occasionally nodding or smiling at familiar stories. They were deeply moved by Eleanor's ability to capture the essence of their friendship and its impact on their lives. The discussion that followed was rich with suggestions and encouragement, helping Eleanor refine her narrative to better express the depth of her experiences.

Encouraged by their feedback, Eleanor spent the next few months revising her manuscript, tightening her narratives, and deepening her insights. She also decided to include a few guest passages written by Mia and Sophie, allowing them to voice their perspectives and enrich the book's diversity of views.

Finally, "Seasons of Wisdom" was ready for publication. Eleanor chose to work with a publisher known for its focus on inspirational and motivational literature. The book launch was set in a cozy independent bookstore in their seaside town, a place that had inspired many of the book's reflections.

The launch day was a celebration not just of Eleanor's accomplishment but of the enduring strength of their friendship. The bookstore was filled with friends, family, and members of Eleanor's blog community, all eager to support her new endeavor.

Eleanor gave a heartfelt speech, acknowledging Mia and Sophie's significant roles in her life. "This book is more than my story; it's a tribute to the power of friendship, the wisdom of experience, and the courage to embrace life's seasons," she shared, her eyes glistening with emotion.

"Seasons of Wisdom" was well-received, resonating with readers from all walks of life. It not only sold well but also sparked discussions and workshops around the themes it explored. Eleanor was invited to speak at various events and panels, where she shared her journey and promoted a positive outlook on aging and personal growth.

As Eleanor continued her new chapter as an author and speaker, she remained closely connected with

Mia and Sophie. Their friendship, tested and strengthened by time and trials, had proven to be an unshakeable foundation in their lives, inspiring each of them to pursue their passions with the support of one another.

CHAPTER 27:

MIA'S TECH EXPANSION

Mia's startup had firmly established itself as a leader in ethical technology, driven by her unwavering commitment to data privacy and user empowerment. Her successful platform had attracted significant attention in the tech world, leading to partnerships with major corporations and invitations to speak at international conferences. However, Mia had bigger plans—she was ready to expand her technological reach into new markets.

As Mia prepared to launch a new product aimed at enhancing cybersecurity for small businesses, she invited Eleanor and Sophie to a strategy session at her office. Their insights had always been valuable, providing unique perspectives that enriched Mia's approach to technology and business development.

During the session, Mia outlined the features of the

new cybersecurity tool, emphasizing its user-friendly design and robust security measures. "I want to make advanced security accessible to small business owners who might not have the resources for large IT departments," Mia explained, showcasing prototypes and initial user feedback.

Eleanor, ever the educator, suggested developing a complementary educational module to help business owners understand the importance of cybersecurity. "It's not just about providing tools; it's about educating your users so they can make informed decisions," she noted.

Sophie, inspired by the discussions, proposed creating a series of promotional videos that could illustrate the dangers of cyber threats through visual storytelling. "Let's make the risks clear and the solutions accessible," she said, sketching rough ideas for the video series.

Encouraged by their enthusiasm and support, Mia finalized her plans for the product launch. The cybersecurity tool was introduced at a major tech conference, with Eleanor and Sophie in attendance. Mia's presentation was compelling, effectively communicating the tool's benefits and the company's commitment to ethical practices.

The launch was a success, garnering interest from various businesses and media outlets. Post-launch, Mia's company offered webinars and workshops, led by Eleanor, to educate business owners about cybersecurity. Sophie's promotional videos were featured on the company's website and social media, helping to explain complex security concepts in an engaging and understandable way.

As her company grew, Mia continued to innovate. Her next project involved developing AI-driven analytics to help businesses understand consumer behavior without compromising privacy. This initiative was in line with her ongoing commitment to ethical tech development, ensuring that consumer data was used responsibly and transparently.

Mia's influence in the tech industry grew, and she was often cited as a pioneer in ethical technology. Her achievements not only elevated her career but also set new standards in the tech community, influencing how companies approached data privacy and consumer rights.

Back at home, as Mia shared her experiences with Eleanor and Sophie over dinner, she reflected on how their friendships had shaped her approach to business. "Your support and insights have been instrumental in my journey. I couldn't have expanded my vision without you both," Mia said, raising a glass to her friends.

Eleanor and Sophie were proud of Mia's accomplishments and how they had contributed in their own ways. Their collaboration had proven that when diverse skills and perspectives came together, the potential for innovation was boundless.

CHAPTER 28:

SOPHIE'S GLOBAL IMPACT

S ophie's artistic journey had taken a significant turn following her travels and the successful exhibitions that captured the essence of her experiences abroad. Her sabbatical not only enriched her personal growth but also broadened her professional network, leading to an invitation to participate in a global art project aimed at raising awareness about climate change.

This new venture, called "Art for Earth," involved artists from various disciplines collaborating to create impactful works that highlighted environmental issues. The project was ambitious, spanning multiple countries and involving interactive installations, public workshops, and collaborative pieces designed to engage communities and provoke meaningful conversations about sustainability.

Sophie was tasked with creating a series of large-scale murals in major cities around the world, each depicting local environmental challenges and the community's relationship with nature. Her first mural, located in Sydney, Australia, depicted the Great Barrier Reef—both its breathtaking beauty and its tragic bleaching, drawing public attention to the urgent need for marine conservation.

As she worked on the mural, Sophie documented her process through a series of vlogs, which she shared on her blog and social media. Her posts garnered significant attention, sparking discussions about coral conservation and sustainable tourism practices. The project's interactive element allowed viewers to scan a QR code at the mural site, leading them to a website with information on how to support local conservation efforts.

Mia and Eleanor followed Sophie's progress closely, offering feedback and promoting her work within their networks. Mia, in particular, facilitated a partnership with a tech company specializing in augmented reality to create an interactive experience for Sophie's murals. Viewers could use their smartphones to see animated effects that illustrated the potential future of these ecosystems, depending on human impact.

Eleanor, leveraging her growing influence as a speaker and author, organized a series of talks at community centers and schools near each mural location. These talks focused on the importance of art in social change, using Sophie's murals as a case study to inspire young artists and activists.

Sophie's next murals in Tokyo, New York, and Rio de Janeiro each addressed local issues—urban air quality, waste management, and deforestation, respectively. Each piece was well-received, drawing local and international media coverage, which further amplified the project's message and Sophie's reputation as an artist deeply committed to social and environmental issues.

The culmination of the "Art for Earth" project was a conference held in Geneva, where artists, activists, and policymakers gathered to discuss the role of art in environmental advocacy. Sophie was invited to speak about her murals and the global response to them. Her presentation highlighted the power of visual storytelling in fostering a deeper understanding and commitment to environmental issues.

After the conference, Sophie returned home, her heart full of the impact she had made and the connections she had forged. A reunion with Mia and Eleanor was filled with joy and pride as they celebrated her achievements and the profound influence of their collaborative efforts.

Their conversation that evening revolved around future projects and the endless possibilities that their unique blend of talents could achieve. As they sat overlooking the ocean, the same sea that had inspired many of Sophie's murals, they planned their next steps, each motivated by the others' successes and energized by their shared commitment to making a difference.

CHAPTER 29:

THE CELEBRATION

 fter Sophie's impactful participation in the "Art for Earth" project and her series of global murals, the trio—Mia, Eleanor, and Sophie— decided to host a joint celebration. This event would not only celebrate Sophie's artistic achievements but also honor Mia's success with her ethical tech startup and Eleanor's impactful launch of her book, "Seasons of Wisdom." They chose to hold the celebration in their hometown, where their friendship had first blossomed, bringing together friends, family, and community members who had supported them along their journeys.

The celebration was planned to be held at the local community center, which had become a hub of their collaborative projects and personal milestones. Mia took charge of incorporating technology into the event, setting up digital displays that interacted with guests to showcase the trio's achievements through interactive timelines and multimedia presentations. She also arranged for a live streaming of the event to include colleagues, friends, and followers from around the world who couldn't attend in person.

Sophie, leveraging her artistic skills, transformed the venue into a visual journey through her murals. Replicas of her art adorned the walls, accompanied by QR codes that guests could scan to view videos of her creative process and the murals' impacts on the communities they were painted in. She also arranged a small gallery of her latest pieces inspired by her travels, available for sale with proceeds going to environmental charities.

Eleanor, ever the educator and speaker, organized a series of short talks for the event. These talks included topics on the power of community and the arts, the role of technology in promoting social good, and the importance of embracing change at any stage of life. She invited local leaders, educators, and young students to speak, fostering a sense of community and shared learning.

As the celebration day arrived, the community center buzzed with excitement. The venue was filled with laughter, music, and the murmurs of impressed guests interacting with the installations. Friends and family expressed their admiration for the trio's accomplishments, while younger attendees felt inspired by the tangible examples of how passion and perseverance could lead to meaningful change.

During the event, Mia, Sophie, and Eleanor each took a moment to address the gathering. They shared their individual stories, emphasizing how their friendship and mutual support had been crucial to overcoming the challenges they faced. They expressed gratitude to their community for its enduring support and encouraged everyone to think about how they could make a difference in their own ways.

The highlight of the evening was the unveiling of a new collaborative project initiated by the trio—a local initiative called "Creativity for Change." This program was designed to mentor young women in technology, arts, and entrepreneurship, providing workshops, resources, and support to help them develop their own projects that addressed local and global challenges.

As the celebration wound down, guests left with a sense of empowerment and a deep appreciation for the power of community and collaboration. Mia, Sophie, and Eleanor stayed back, reflecting on the evening and discussing the future of their new initiative. They were excited about the potential to impact lives and were committed to being actively involved.

Their friendship had blossomed into a powerful partnership, driving change and inspiring those around them. As they locked up the community center, they knew that this celebration was just another beginning in their continuous journey of growth and impact.

CHAPTER 30:

CREATIVITY FOR CHANGE

T he "Creativity for Change" initiative quickly became a cornerstone of Mia, Sophie, and Eleanor's collaborative efforts, blending their passions and expertise to foster a new generation of changemakers. The program aimed to empower young women in their community by providing mentorship in technology, the arts, and entrepreneurship, with a special focus on projects that addressed social and environmental issues.

As the program kicked off, the trio approached local schools, universities, and community groups to recruit participants. They designed a curriculum that included workshops on digital literacy, art creation, business fundamentals, and project management. The goal was not only to educate but also to inspire these young women to think creatively about solutions to real-world problems.

Mia leveraged her tech network to bring in guest speakers and set up internships, giving participants firsthand experience in the tech industry. She also developed a module on ethical technology practices, ensuring that the young women understood the importance of considering the societal impacts of tech innovations.

Sophie, drawing on her global art experiences, led workshops on using art as a tool for social change. She guided participants through the process of conceptualizing and creating art pieces that communicated powerful messages about issues such as climate change, social justice, and community resilience. Her sessions included hands-on activities in various mediums, from traditional painting to digital art and mixed media.

Eleanor utilized her experience as an educator and author to teach effective communication and leadership skills. Her sessions focused on how to articulate ideas clearly, write compelling grant proposals, and present projects to potential backers. She also shared lessons from her book, emphasizing the value of persistence, adaptability, and empathy in personal and professional growth.

The program culminated in a community showcase where participants presented their projects to an audience of local leaders, potential investors, and family members. The projects ranged from a smartphone app that helped users reduce their carbon footprint to a social media campaign that raised awareness about mental health resources for teenagers.

The showcase was a resounding success, with several participants receiving offers of support to further develop their projects. The local press covered the event, highlighting the positive impact of "Creativity for Change" on the community and the innovative approaches taken by the participants.

Encouraged by the success of the first cohort, Mia, Sophie, and Eleanor planned to expand the program. They sought additional funding and partnerships to offer more frequent sessions and to possibly replicate the model in other communities. Their vision was to create a network of young women empowered to use technology and art to make a difference in the world.

As they discussed these plans at their regular meeting spot by the sea, the trio reflected on how their own journey of friendship and collaboration had sparked this impactful initiative. They were proud of the role they had played in mentoring the next generation and excited about the future of "Creativity for Change."

"Look how far we've come," Mia mused, watching

the waves crash onto the shore. "And yet, it feels like we're just getting started."

Sophie nodded in agreement, her eyes bright with enthusiasm. "Every end is just a new beginning, right?"

Eleanor smiled, her gaze sweeping over her friends. "Exactly. And as long as we have each other, there's no limit to what we can accomplish."

Together, they looked out at the sea, inspired by the endless horizon and the infinite possibilities that lay ahead.

CHAPTER 31:

EXPANDING HORIZONS

E ncouraged by the success of the first cohort of "Creativity for Change," Mia, Sophie, and Eleanor were keen to see how much further they could take their initiative. Their next goal was not just to expand the program locally but to establish branches in other regions, potentially even internationally, to inspire and empower a broader audience.

Mia, leveraging her connections in the tech industry, initiated talks with potential partners and sponsors who could provide both funding and technology resources. Her aim was to create digital hubs where young women around the world could access the "Creativity for Change" curriculum online, participate in virtual workshops, and connect with mentors through a dedicated platform.

Sophie focused on curating a traveling art exhibit featuring works created by participants of the program. These artworks highlighted various global issues, showcasing the unique perspectives and creativity of young women from diverse backgrounds. The exhibit was designed to not only raise awareness but also to generate funding for the initiative through art sales.

Eleanor, drawing upon her experience as a published author and speaker, worked on developing a series of educational materials and books that could be used in conjunction with the workshops. These resources were aimed at guiding participants in developing their projects and enhancing their leadership skills. She also planned a series of speaking tours to promote the initiative and share success stories from the participants.

As plans progressed, the trio organized a webinar to officially launch the global expansion of "Creativity for Change." The event featured testimonials from past participants, demonstrations of projects that had been developed through the program, and a detailed presentation of the new digital platform.

The launch was a significant success, attracting attention from educational institutions, NGOs, and corporations interested in partnering with the initiative. This support enabled the trio to plan for the setup of local chapters in various cities around the world, each tailored to address the specific needs and challenges of those communities.

With the global network growing, Mia, Sophie, and Eleanor established a central team to manage the initiative, ensuring that the core values of creativity, empowerment, and change remained at the heart of all activities. They also recruited local leaders to run the chapters, providing training and resources to ensure consistency and impact.

As the first international chapters began their activities, the feedback was overwhelmingly positive. Participants appreciated the hands-on approach and the opportunity to work on meaningful projects. Success stories from various chapters were shared on the initiative's website and social media, inspiring a new wave of young women to join the program.

During a review meeting, Mia, Sophie, and Eleanor were overjoyed by the progress but also mindful of the challenges ahead. "We need to ensure we're not just expanding, but also deepening the impact," Mia noted, emphasizing the importance of continuous improvement.

Sophie suggested incorporating more environmental projects, given the increasing concerns about climate change. Eleanor agreed, adding that leadership development should continue to be a central focus, empowering participants to take on influential roles in their communities.

As they planned for the future, the trio celebrated the journey of "Creativity for Change" from a local workshop series to an international movement. They knew the road ahead would require dedication and adaptation, but they were ready for the challenge, driven by their mission to empower the next generation of women leaders.

CHAPTER 32:

A NEW CHAPTER BEGINS

As "Creativity for Change" continued to expand globally, the trio—Mia, Sophie, and Eleanor— decided to delve deeper into individual projects within the initiative that showcased significant impact or innovation. One such project was led by a participant named Lara, a young woman from a local chapter in Nairobi, Kenya. Lara had developed a unique approach to recycling and waste management that not only addressed environmental concerns but also empowered local communities economically.

Lara's project, called "Re-Canvas," utilized discarded materials to create functional art pieces and home decor products. By training local artisans and unemployed youth in her community to craft these items, she not only promoted environmental sustainability but also provided valuable skills and employment opportunities. Her initiative had caught the attention of the trio because of its holistic approach to problem-solving and community engagement.

Seeing the potential for wider application and wanting to support Lara's efforts, Sophie flew to Nairobi to collaborate directly with her. Together, they worked on integrating more artistic elements into the products, enhancing their appeal and marketability. Sophie's experience and visibility helped bring international attention to "Re-Canvas," attracting potential buyers and investors.

Meanwhile, Mia focused on developing a digital platform specifically for projects like Lara's that needed a broader audience and access to e-commerce solutions. This platform was designed not only to help sell the products made by these community projects but also to tell their stories, connecting consumers with the artisans and their environmental and social missions.

Eleanor, inspired by Lara's story and others like it, began writing a series of articles and a potential follow-up book focusing on the powerful narratives of young women around the world who were leading change in their communities. She highlighted how "Creativity for Change" had become a catalyst for these leaders, providing them with the tools and support needed to bring their ideas to fruition.

As "Re-Canvas" gained momentum, Lara was invited to speak at international conferences, sharing her insights and the success of her project. Sophie's collaboration with her continued, with both working on expanding the product line and exploring new materials and techniques. Their joint efforts were not only beneficial in terms of business but also strengthened the bond between the global chapters of "Creativity for Change."

The success of Lara's project led to the establishment of a special fund within "Creativity for Change" aimed at supporting similar sustainability initiatives led by young women. This fund helped to seed new projects, providing the initial capital and resources needed to get off the ground.

As Mia, Sophie, and Eleanor gathered at the annual "Creativity for Change" summit, they reflected on the growth of the initiative and the individual stories of change and innovation. They discussed plans to further enhance mentorship and support structures, ensuring that more young women like Lara could realize their potential and make a tangible impact on their communities.

The trio's dedication to fostering creativity and change had rippled across the globe, creating a network of empowered young women leaders. As they looked to the future, they were filled with hope and determination, committed to continuing their support and to witnessing the unfolding of many more chapters of transformation.

CHAPTER 33:

NURTURING GLOBAL LEADERS

As "Creativity for Change" flourished, so did the variety and impact of its projects, each led by young women with visions to transform their communities. To enhance this burgeoning network,

Mia, Sophie, and Eleanor decided to create a leadership program specifically designed to nurture and support these young leaders. This new initiative, called the "Global Leaders Program," was crafted to provide advanced training, networking opportunities, and individual mentorship tailored to the unique challenges these women faced.

The inaugural session of the "Global Leaders Program" was set to take place in a serene location in Costa Rica, chosen for its rich biodiversity and successful community-based conservation efforts, which aligned perfectly with many of the initiative's sustainability projects. The program invited leaders from various "Creativity for Change" chapters, including Lara from Nairobi, to participate in an intensive two-week workshop.

Mia developed the curriculum, which included modules on technological solutions for social issues, ethical business practices, and advanced project management. She utilized her tech network to bring in experts and innovators as guest speakers, ensuring that the participants had access to cutting-edge knowledge and experiences.

Sophie took charge of the creative aspects of the program, organizing sessions on art as a tool for social engagement and environmental advocacy. She incorporated field trips to local art collectives and conservation sites, where participants could see firsthand how integrated community efforts led to impactful change.

Eleanor, leveraging her experience as an author and educator, focused on communication and leadership skills. She conducted workshops on effective storytelling, public speaking, and writing, crucial skills for the young leaders to advocate for their projects and secure funding and support.

The program also included a significant networking component, encouraging participants to form lasting connections with each other. These relationships would build a supportive global network, fostering collaborations and shared resources across different regions and cultures.

Lara, inspired by the program, deepened her understanding of sustainable materials and expanded her "Re-Canvas" project. She collaborated with a fellow participant from Brazil, who introduced her to new techniques for using recycled plastics in art and product design. Together, they planned a pilot project to implement these techniques in both their communities, supported by the sustainability fund established by "Creativity for Change."

As the two-week program concluded, each participant presented their enhanced project plan to a panel of experienced entrepreneurs and activists. The feedback was overwhelmingly positive, with several projects receiving additional funding and support.

The success of the "Global Leaders Program" prompted Mia, Sophie, and Eleanor to plan annual sessions, each to be held in different locations around the world to highlight various challenges and innovations. The program quickly became a cornerstone of "Creativity for Change," celebrated for its role in empowering young women to become leaders in their fields.

Reflecting on the impact of their initiative, the trio felt immense pride and a renewed sense of purpose. They continued to innovate and expand their efforts, driven by the belief that empowering young women with creativity and technology could lead to significant global change.

CHAPTER 34:

BRIDGING COMMUNITIES

I nspired by the success of the "Global Leaders Program" and the palpable impact of projects like Lara's "Re-Canvas," Mia, Sophie, and Eleanor sought to further enhance "Creativity for Change" by launching a new initiative called "Bridging Communities." This program aimed to foster direct exchanges between different chapters, allowing participants to share experiences, learn from each other's successes and challenges, and collaboratively develop solutions that could be adapted across diverse geographical and cultural contexts.

The first exchange was organized between the chapters in Nairobi and Rio de Janeiro. These two vibrant cities, although continents apart, shared similar urban environmental challenges, including waste management and community health issues related to pollution. The program facilitated a series of virtual workshops where participants from each city presented their ongoing projects and discussed their local environments.

Sophie led a creative workshop focused on using art to raise awareness and engage local communities. She introduced techniques that had been effective in her travels and exhibitions, encouraging participants to adapt these to their local cultures and issues. This exchange inspired a collaborative mural project, where artists from both chapters co-created pieces that were displayed in both cities, symbolizing their shared commitment to environmental sustainability.

Mia, leveraging her technological expertise, facilitated a session on using low-cost technology to enhance project efficiency and reach. This included training on building simple apps for community reporting of environmental hazards, which were particularly relevant for the Rio chapter, where community monitoring had become an essential part of their environmental advocacy.

Eleanor conducted leadership and communication workshops, focusing on how to effectively advocate for policy changes and engage stakeholders. Her sessions included training on negotiation techniques, public speaking, and the use of digital platforms to amplify their voices. These skills were crucial for the Nairobi chapter, which was working closely with local government bodies to implement waste recycling initiatives.

As "Bridging Communities" evolved, more exchanges were organized, involving chapters from different parts of the world, each focusing on unique themes such as water conservation, renewable energy projects, and digital literacy for underserved communities. These exchanges not only enhanced the projects but also built a strong network of informed and empowered leaders who supported each other.

The success stories from these exchanges were compiled into an annual "Creativity for Change" impact report, which highlighted the innovative solutions developed and the tangible improvements in the communities involved. This report was shared widely through Mia's tech networks, Sophie's art exhibitions, and Eleanor's speaking engagements, drawing more support and recognition for the initiative.

Reflecting on the growth and success of "Bridging Communities," the trio planned a global summit to bring together participants from all chapters. This event was intended to celebrate the achievements of the past year, share best practices, and plan future collaborative projects.

As they prepared for the summit, Mia, Sophie, and Eleanor were filled with a profound sense of accomplishment and anticipation. Their vision had ignited a global movement, transforming "Creativity for Change" into a beacon of innovation, empowerment, and global cooperation. They looked forward to witnessing the continuing evolution of their initiative, confident in the knowledge that together, they were making a world of difference.

CHAPTER 35:

GLOBAL SUMMIT AND FUTURE VISIONS

T he inaugural "Creativity for Change" global summit was set to be a landmark event, drawing participants from every chapter around the world to a picturesque location in Greece, chosen for its historical significance as a crossroads of civilizations and ideas. The summit aimed to celebrate the achievements of the initiative, foster deeper connections among the participants, and outline strategies for the future.

Mia, Sophie, and Eleanor arrived a few days early to oversee the preparations. The venue was an open-air amphitheater overlooking the Mediterranean, a symbolic setting that underscored the theme of interconnectedness and collective action. As they walked through the venue, checking every detail, the trio felt a mix of excitement and nostalgia, reflecting on the journey that had brought them to this point.

The summit opened with a keynote speech by Eleanor, who shared the story of "Creativity for Change" from its inception to its current global impact. Her speech highlighted the transformational stories of participants like Lara and underscored the initiative's role in empowering young women to become leaders and innovators in their communities.

Following the keynote, Mia led a panel discussion on the integration of technology in social projects. She showcased examples from the "Bridging Communities" exchanges, demonstrating how technological solutions had enhanced project outcomes and engagement. The discussion also explored upcoming technological trends and how they could be harnessed to further the goals of "Creativity for Change."

Sophie moderated a workshop on creative activism, where participants shared how art had played a crucial role in their projects. This session included interactive segments, where attendees collaborated on a large-scale art installation that depicted the summit's themes. This artwork was planned to travel to each participant's home city after the summit, symbolizing their shared commitment and collective impact.

One of the summit's highlights was the "Future Visions" brainstorming session, where participants were encouraged to propose new project ideas and expansions. This session generated a wealth of ideas, from a mobile app connecting global eco-activists to a mentorship program linking young innovators with seasoned entrepreneurs and activists.

The closing ceremony of the summit featured a commitment pledge, where each chapter committed to specific goals for the coming year. These goals were ambitious yet achievable, reflecting the collective aspiration of the network to make a tangible impact on global issues.

As the summit concluded, the participants returned to their communities, energized and equipped with new tools, ideas, and support networks. Mia, Sophie, and Eleanor stayed behind to discuss the outcomes and plan the next steps. They agreed to establish a permanent secretariat to coordinate the initiative's activities and support the chapters more effectively.

Reflecting on the summit and the path ahead, the trio felt a profound sense of pride and responsibility. "We started this as a small project to empower young women in our community," Mia mused as they watched the sunset over the Mediterranean. "Now, it's a global movement. It's incredible how far we've come and how much further we can go."

Sophie added, "It's like planting seeds. We've planted ideas and passion across the world, and now we get to watch them grow and blossom."

Eleanor concluded, "And as they grow, so do we. Every challenge, every success teaches us more about the world and ourselves. The journey continues."

As they planned for the future, Mia, Sophie, and Eleanor looked forward to seeing how "Creativity for Change" would evolve, confident that their continued collaboration would inspire further innovation and transformation worldwide.

CHAPTER 36:

INNOVATIONS AND INSPIRATIONS

R einvigorated by the success of the "Creativity for Change" global summit, Mia, Sophie, and Eleanor returned home filled with new ideas and a renewed sense of purpose. They decided to focus on implementing some of the most promising projects discussed during the "Future Visions" brainstorming session, particularly those that aligned closely with their individual passions and expertise.

Mia's New Venture:

Mia was particularly inspired by the idea of a mobile app that connected eco-activists globally. She saw the potential for technology to not only bridge geographical distances but also to streamline the sharing of resources and strategies. With her tech startup running smoothly and a competent team in place, Mia felt ready to tackle this new challenge. She began by assembling a small, dedicated team to develop the app, named "EcoConnect."

Her vision for "EcoConnect" was an intuitive platform where users could share successful case studies, upcoming environmental events, and innovative sustainability projects. The app would also include a feature to coordinate global actions, such as synchronized tree planting days or international webinars on climate change.

Sophie's Artistic Collaborations:

Sophie was moved by the collaborative art installation at the summit and decided to expand on this concept. She envisioned a series of international art installations, each created by artists from different backgrounds but centered on common themes of unity and environmental conservation.

Her first project, "Canvas of Continents," involved artists from six continents who would each design a piece of a larger mosaic. These pieces would be united at a central exhibition, symbolically and physically, to form a single, cohesive artwork. This project not only celebrated cultural diversity but also highlighted the universal importance of protecting our planet.

Eleanor's Educational Initiatives:

Eleanor was excited about a proposal for an international mentorship program for young women aspiring to be leaders in their communities.

Drawing on her experience as an author and educator, Eleanor began outlining a curriculum that included leadership development, effective communication, and project management.

She reached out to universities and women's organizations to partner in this initiative, aiming to pair experienced mentors with emerging leaders. The program, "Leaders of Tomorrow," was designed to be flexible, accommodating the different needs and schedules of its participants, but with a strong foundation in nurturing capable, confident leaders.

Bringing Their Projects Together:

As these projects took shape, Mia, Sophie, and Eleanor found ways to intertwine their efforts. "EcoConnect" featured promotions for Sophie's "Canvas of Continents" exhibitions and provided a platform for participants in Eleanor's "Leaders of Tomorrow" to share their experiences and seek advice.

A few months later, they organized a joint event where they showcased the progress of their projects. The event was streamed on "EcoConnect," featured artwork from "Canvas of Continents," and included a panel discussion with some of the first graduates of the "Leaders of Tomorrow" program.

The community response was overwhelmingly

positive, with many expressing admiration for how seamlessly the projects integrated and amplified each other. For Mia, Sophie, and Eleanor, the event was a poignant reminder of how their individual passions and efforts could come together to create something greater than the sum of its parts.

Reflecting on their journey, the trio planned to continue their collaborative efforts, each driven by the belief that their united vision could inspire change across the world.

CHAPTER 37:

ECOCONNECT'S GLOBAL IMPACT

s Mia's "EcoConnect" app began to gain traction, its influence extended far beyond its initial scope, becoming a pivotal tool in the global environmental movement. The app's success was a testament to Mia's foresight in leveraging technology for social good, and it catalyzed a series of impactful collaborations and initiatives across the world.

Expansion and Enhancement:

Mia focused on continuously enhancing "EcoConnect," incorporating feedback from its growing user base. One significant update was the integration of real-time environmental data feeds, allowing users to monitor local air quality, water safety, and weather conditions. This feature made the app not just a platform for communication but also a crucial resource for environmental awareness and safety.

Strategic Partnerships:

To expand the app's reach and capabilities, Mia forged partnerships with major environmental NGOs and research institutions. These partnerships provided "EcoConnect" with valuable content and credibility, helping to attract a wider audience. They also facilitated unique campaigns, such as global biodiversity challenges where users could participate in local conservation activities and share their efforts on the platform.

Community Projects Spotlight:

"EcoConnect" also featured a section dedicated to showcasing innovative community-led projects around the world. This spotlight helped small-scale initiatives gain international attention and funding. One such project was a mangrove restoration program in Southeast Asia, which, after being featured on "EcoConnect," received significant contributions from the global community.

Educational Workshops and Webinars:

Leveraging the app's network, Mia organized virtual workshops and webinars led by experts in various environmental fields. These educational sessions covered topics from sustainable urban planning to wildlife conservation techniques, making high-quality environmental education accessible to a global audience.

Integration with "Canvas of Continents":

Sophie's "Canvas of Continents" project benefited significantly from its integration into "EcoConnect." The app provided a virtual gallery space where users could view the installations and learn about the artists and the environmental messages behind their works. This collaboration not only enriched the content on "EcoConnect" but also broadened the audience for Sophie's art, engaging users who might not typically visit art exhibitions.

Supporting "Leaders of Tomorrow":

Eleanor's "Leaders of Tomorrow" program utilized "EcoConnect" to facilitate mentorship connections and to provide a platform for emerging leaders to share their projects and seek community advice. The app's global reach helped these young women gain visibility and support from an international network, enhancing the impact of Eleanor's initiative.

Global Environmental Summit:

Inspired by the success of "EcoConnect" and its role in uniting environmental efforts worldwide, Mia planned a Global Environmental Summit. Hosted virtually on the app, the summit brought together environmental activists, policymakers, scientists, and community leaders to discuss pressing environmental issues and to strategize on global action plans. The event was a milestone, highlighting "EcoConnect" as not just a tool for communication but a global platform for environmental advocacy and action.

As Mia, Sophie, and Eleanor celebrated the achievements of "EcoConnect" at their annual review meeting, they reflected on how each of their projects had interwoven to create a comprehensive tapestry of impact. Their collaborative spirit, driven by a shared commitment to making a difference, had catalyzed change across communities and continents, setting a powerful example of how technology, art, and education could converge to address some of the world's most challenging issues.

CHAPTER 38:

ADVANCING "LEADERS OF TOMORROW"

 A fter the success of the Global Environmental

Summit hosted on Mia's "EcoConnect" app, Eleanor felt inspired to further expand her "Leaders of Tomorrow" mentorship program. Seeing the profound impact that effective leadership and communication could have on environmental and social projects, she envisioned a more integrated approach that could leverage the capabilities of "EcoConnect" and incorporate artistic elements from Sophie's projects.

Expansion Plans:

Eleanor set her sights on transforming "Leaders of Tomorrow" from a primarily local initiative into a global mentorship network. Her goal was to connect young female leaders from around the world, providing them with the resources, skills, and support needed to drive change within their communities.

To achieve this, Eleanor worked closely with Mia to integrate a special mentorship module within the "EcoConnect" platform. This new feature allowed mentors and mentees to connect easily, share resources, and even conduct virtual meetings directly through the app.

Collaborative Workshops:

Sophie contributed to the program by organizing collaborative art and design workshops. These workshops were aimed at helping participants express their project visions creatively, enhancing their public engagement and presentation skills. The artwork produced during these workshops was used in campaign materials for their projects, adding a visually impactful element that drew more attention and support.

Enhanced Training Modules:

Eleanor updated the curriculum to include advanced leadership training, focusing on topics such as strategic planning, sustainability in leadership, and digital communications. Recognizing the importance of adaptability in leadership, she also introduced a series on managing virtual teams and using technology to enhance project outcomes, drawing on Mia's expertise.

Global Leadership Conference:

With the expanded network and enhanced training modules in place, Eleanor planned the first "Leaders of Tomorrow" Global Leadership Conference. The conference was designed to be a hybrid event, with local in-person gatherings linked via "EcoConnect" to a global virtual audience. This format allowed for a wider reach and facilitated an exchange of ideas among young leaders from different cultural and geographical backgrounds.

Conference Highlights:

The conference featured keynote speeches from renowned leaders in business, activism, and academia. Interactive panels discussed pressing global issues such as climate change, gender equality, and technological ethics. Breakout sessions allowed participants to delve into specific areas of interest, receive targeted training, and discuss their projects in detail.

Sophie hosted a special session on "Art as Advocacy," showcasing successful projects where art had played a crucial role in raising awareness and driving public engagement. This session was particularly popular, inspiring many participants to think creatively about using art in their own initiatives.

Outcomes and Impact:

The conference was a resounding success, significantly raising the profile of the "Leaders of Tomorrow" program and resulting in substantial growth in applications for the next cycle of mentorship. Many participants secured funding and partnerships during the conference, empowering them to launch or expand their projects.

As Eleanor, Mia, and Sophie reviewed the conference outcomes, they were thrilled with the progress and impact of their collaborative efforts. They discussed future plans to ensure the sustainability of the "Leaders of Tomorrow" program, exploring new partnerships and funding opportunities to support even more young leaders globally.

Reflecting on their journey, the trio was proud of the dynamic ecosystem they had built, which nurtured and propelled young women to become impactful leaders. They were excited about the future, confident that the network they had created would continue to foster innovation and positive change worldwide.

CHAPTER 39:

NEW HORIZONS IN PERSONAL LIVES

hile the trio's professional projects continued to flourish, important personal milestones also shaped their lives. Each woman faced new challenges and opportunities that reflected their individual growth and the deepening of their friendships.

Mia's New Chapter:

Mia reached a pivotal moment in her personal life when she and Alex decided to get engaged. The decision came after a thoughtful conversation about their future, balancing their careers, and shared values. They planned a small, intimate wedding, focusing on sustainability and community, incorporating many of the principles that Mia championed in her professional life.

In preparation for this new chapter, Mia took a step back to reassess her role at her tech company. She decided to appoint a CEO to handle day-to-day operations while she moved into a strategic advisory role. This shift allowed her more time to focus on personal projects and her upcoming marriage, proving her commitment to maintaining a balance between her professional and personal life.

Sophie's Artistic Retreat:

Inspired by her global travels and the success of her collaborative projects, Sophie chose to take a sabbatical to focus on her personal art. She rented a studio in a quiet countryside location, immersing herself in creating a new solo exhibition titled "Reflections of Change." This collection was deeply personal, exploring themes of identity, growth, and the interplay between human emotions and environmental consciousness.

Sophie's retreat was not only a period of intense artistic productivity but also a time for self-reflection. She documented her journey through a series of blog posts, which resonated deeply with her audience, adding another layer of intimacy and engagement to her work.

Eleanor's Health and Community Engagement:

Eleanor faced a health scare that prompted her to slow down and prioritize her well-being. After a brief hospitalization, she recovered well, thanks in part to the support from Mia and Sophie, who were steadfast in their visits and assistance.

Eleanor's experience with illness inspired her to start a new community initiative focused on senior health and wellness. She organized workshops and seminars in her living community, bringing in experts on senior nutrition, exercise, and mental health. Her initiative quickly gained traction, enhancing her role as a community leader and advocate for healthy aging.

Reunion and Reflection:

After several months apart, Mia, Sophie, and Eleanor reunited at their favorite coastal retreat, where they had shared many pivotal moments throughout their friendship. This reunion was a time to celebrate Mia's upcoming wedding, showcase Sophie's new art pieces, and support Eleanor's health initiative.

The weekend was filled with laughter, stories, and planning for future projects. They discussed the evolving landscape of their lives and careers, acknowledging how each had influenced the others in profound ways. Their discussions also touched on potential collaborative efforts that could integrate Mia's tech expertise, Sophie's artistic vision, and Eleanor's focus on community wellness.

As they watched the sunset over the ocean, the trio reflected on the intricate tapestry of their lives— interwoven with challenges, achievements, and constant support. They realized that no matter the distance or changes in their personal journeys, their friendship remained a cornerstone of their lives, ever dynamic and evolving.

CHAPTER 40:

CELEBRATIONS AND NEW BEGINNINGS

s the date of Mia's wedding approached, the trio was engulfed in a whirlwind of preparations and excitement. Mia and Alex had chosen an eco-friendly venue nestled in a lush forest, reflecting their shared commitment to sustainability and their love for nature. The wedding promised to be a beautiful amalgamation of modern technology and traditional elements, showcasing Mia's professional ethos and personal style.

Mia's Eco-Friendly Wedding:

The wedding was meticulously planned to minimize environmental impact. Invitations were sent digitally via Mia's app, EcoConnect, which also served as a platform for guests to coordinate travel plans to reduce carbon footprints and share accommodations. The decor featured local flowers and reusable materials, and the menu was crafted from locally sourced, organic ingredients.

Sophie contributed to the event by designing the wedding favors—small, potted succulents painted with delicate scenes of nature, each a miniature version of her larger environmental artworks. These gifts were meant not just as mementos but as a reminder of the couple's dedication to environmental stewardship.

Eleanor, drawing on her experience and the wisdom she'd compiled in her book "Seasons of Wisdom," prepared a heartfelt speech for the couple. She spoke about the journey of love and partnership, emphasizing the importance of support and growth both as individuals and as a couple.

Sophie's Artistic Ventures:

Fresh from her sabbatical and inspired by the preparations for Mia's wedding, Sophie decided to launch a new series of workshops called "Art &

Soul." These workshops were designed to help individuals explore their creativity in relation to their personal and environmental connections. Held in her new countryside studio, the workshops quickly gained popularity, attracting not just aspiring artists but anyone seeking a deeper connection with nature and their inner selves.

Sophie also began planning her next major exhibition, "Echoes of the Earth," which would feature the artworks she had created during her retreat. The exhibition was set to tour several cities, bringing her message of environmental consciousness and artistic expression to a broader audience.

Eleanor's Community Impact:

Energized by the success of her health and wellness initiative, Eleanor expanded her program to include more comprehensive topics such as mental health, digital literacy for seniors, and intergenerational communication. She partnered with local health experts and tech volunteers to create a series of engaging seminars and interactive sessions.

The positive feedback from her community fueled Eleanor's passion further, prompting her to start writing a second book focused on healthy aging and community involvement. This new project aimed to provide practical advice and inspirational stories to empower seniors worldwide.

A Joyous Reunion:

Mia's wedding day arrived, a joyful celebration that brought together friends, family, and colleagues in a picturesque setting. The ceremony was a beautiful testament to the couple's journey and their shared values. Mia, Sophie, and Eleanor shared a special moment during the festivities, reflecting on their enduring friendship and how it had sustained and enriched their lives.

As the evening wound down, the trio stood together, watching the stars emerge in the clear night sky, their hearts full of joy and gratitude for the paths they had traversed together. They talked excitedly about the future, ready to face new challenges and adventures, knowing that their bond would continue to inspire and support them.

Made in the USA
Las Vegas, NV
07 December 2024